I0731541

her airman

A LOVE GAMES NOVEL
by
ALLYSON LINDT

This book is a work of fiction.

While reference might be made to actual historical events or existing locations, the names, characters, places and incidents are either the product of the author's imagination or are used fictitiously, and any resemblance to actual persons, living or dead, business establishments, events, or locales is entirely coincidental.

Manufactured in the United States of America
Acelette Press

For my eternal dragon

chapter zero

CharcoalDreams: What's with the new screen name?

InvaderZ: Apparently The Taurus made a couple of HS watch lists—got to be too much of a hassle to mask myself. Fucking Air Force firewalls.

CharcoalDreams: First computer when you were five, hacking since you were seven, and in the fifteen years since then, you've never backed down from a network security challenge. You don't mean high school, do you?

InvaderZ: Homeland Security.

CharcoalDreams: Of course :-P InvaderZ-do you pronounce it like the video game?

InvaderZ: You pronounce it like Invader Zee—two words.

CharcoalDreams: :-D Right, cuz Z for Zane, I get it. So what are you up to?

InvaderZ: You really want to know?

CharcoalDreams: I asked, didn't I?

InvaderZ: Yeah, but this is different.

CharcoalDreams: ??? I thought we could tell each other anything.

InvaderZ: Yeah, but this is different.

CharcoalDreams: Not funny. You could have just said *nothing* and I would have dropped it. But you had to make it sound interesting.

InvaderZ: Fine. I was considering jerking off.

CharcoalDreams:…

InvaderZ: Told you that you didn't want to hear it.

CharcoalDreams: You caught me off guard is all. I mean I figure, you being all *my girlfriend left me and I'll never sleep with another woman again* that you were getting off somehow. I just didn't put a lot of thought into it.

InvaderZ: Now I feel awkward.

CharcoalDreams: You shouldn't have brought it up then.

InvaderZ: You've never put any thought into it, but I'm picturing you naked all the time.

CharcoalDreams: :-O You are not.

InvaderZ: Well, not all the time. But you've made an appearance in the mental rotation. Just because you're my best friend doesn't mean I've never noticed how drop-dead sexy you look in cutoffs. Or a bikini. Or one of my T-shirts and nothing else. Wait, that one was all in my head.

CharcoalDreams: Do you know this is getting awkward?

InvaderZ: You started it.

CharcoalDreams: I did not.

InvaderZ: Whatever. Forget I mentioned it.

CharcoalDreams: Do I ever *start it* in these fantasies of yours?

InvaderZ: I thought you wanted to drop it.

CharcoalDreams: Now you have me thinking about it.

InvaderZ: Sometimes.

CharcoalDreams: Sometimes…I start it?

InvaderZ: Yup. Sometimes I ask you, sometimes you ask me, we screw, it's all good.

CharcoalDreams: That's it.

InvaderZ: What?

CharcoalDreams: *We screw, it's all good.* That's about the weakest fantasy I've ever heard.

InvaderZ: So, no offense, Riley. But I'm a guy. If I can imagine myself sticking my dick in something warm and attractive, I don't need a lot more.

CharcoalDreams: So crude.

InvaderZ: At least I let you make an appearance. You never even think about me.

CharcoalDreams: If I did, it'd be a much more elaborate fantasy. You at least deserve that.

InvaderZ: Like what?

CharcoalDreams: I don't know, but it needs build-up, and tension, and fun, and intimacy.

InvaderZ: You do too know.

CharcoalDreams: Excuse me?

InvaderZ: You wouldn't have said it if you didn't have an idea. You've obviously created these elaborate fantasies before. Would it destroy you to write me into one?

CharcoalDreams:…

InvaderZ: ?

CharcoalDreams: Since that's pretty much what my brain has been doing since you brought it up I'm going to say it wouldn't destroy me at all.

InvaderZ: Are you complaining?

CharcoalDreams: I guess it all depends on how good my imagination thinks you are in the sack.

InvaderZ: Just don't make it too impossible a dream to live up to.

CharcoalDreams: You're thousands of miles away and will be for at least the next five years. When are you going to get a chance to live up to it? Besides,

I'd never let it screw up our friendship, and you've already sworn you're going to be celibate for the rest of your life.

InvaderZ: In that case, make sure I'm absolutely fantastic. And describe it to me in vivid detail.

CharcoalDreams: I thought you didn't need an elaborate fantasy, just a mental image of something…what was it ~scrolls up~ warm and attractive?

InvaderZ: Just because I don't need it doesn't mean I don't like the idea. Teach me the error of my ways, oh wise one. Tell me how imaginary me is going to make you scream my name in ecstasy.

CharcoalDreams: I don't know, um…You come over to watch movies.

InvaderZ: And that's sexy?

CharcoalDreams: And that's how it starts. The first hint of sexy is that you're wearing a battered T-shirt that's just the right amount of soft, that smells like you, and ripped jeans. And we're probably drinking a little, not enough to get drunk, just a beer each or something, and you're letting me curl up against you on the couch like we did back in high school.

InvaderZ: But you've never thought about this before. And then we screw?

CharcoalDreams: Eventually. Give it time.

InvaderZ: Sorry. But tonight would be nice.

CharcoalDreams: :-P And since we're watching

cable—HBO or Showtime or something—and it's late, some stupid, R-rated fake porn movie comes on.

InvaderZ: I hate those things.

CharcoalDreams: I know. Anyway, we start joking about how ridiculously censored they are, and even pretending to act out certain scenes, and all the sudden, you've got me on my stomach, straddling me, arms pinned behind my back.

InvaderZ: Nice. Actually really, really hot. I should warn you, if you keep going, I'm going to jerk off.

CharcoalDreams: I didn't need to know that.

InvaderZ: Why not? I'd want to know if you were.

CharcoalDreams:…I was thinking about it.

InvaderZ: Wait, really?

CharcoalDreams: ~blush~ seriously.

InvaderZ: Because I'd much rather hear about that.

CharcoalDreams: What do you want to know?

InvaderZ: God damn it, why can't my bandwidth support video?

CharcoalDreams: I guess you'll have to use your imagination. Say you could watch, what would you want to see?

InvaderZ: What are you wearing?

CharcoalDreams: Cliché, but I'll bite. T-shirt and jeans.

InvaderZ: You're not even trying. Take your shirt off.

CharcoalDreams: Mmm…bossy. I like it.

InvaderZ: I'll keep that in mind.

CharcoalDreams: Shirt's off. Now I'm topless except for this red lace bra that's probably a half-cup too small, so my boobs are kind of…pushing to get out.

InvaderZ: Better. You should oblige at least one of them. I've always wondered what your tits looked like.

CharcoalDreams: You know, round, fun to play with, and right now with very swollen, pink nipples.

InvaderZ: Since I can't be there to do it myself, you should play with them. Pinch your nipples, roll them between your fingers. Make yourself moan.

CharcoalDreams: ~moans~ do you want me to lick one, too?

InvaderZ: You can do that? Fuck yes.

CharcoalDreams: Too bad I don't have anything else here to use my tongue on.

InvaderZ: I'm so hard right now. Are you getting wet?

CharcoalDreams: ~squirms in seat~ Presumably.

InvaderZ: You should probably lose your jeans so you can do a hands-on test.

CharcoalDreams: Is that an order?

InvaderZ: Yes.

CharcoalDreams: I like this a lot. So now you have me stripped down to my lacy things, and two fingers sliding easily between my legs confirms that, yes, you've got me very wet.

InvaderZ: Incredible. Do you still have that vibrator?

CharcoalDreams: How do you know about that?

InvaderZ: I'd say lucky guess, but you don't always tuck it away as well as you think you do. Grab it.

CharcoalDreams: Yes, Sir.

InvaderZ: In this fantasy of yours, I get to pin your arms behind your back, strip away your clothes, and have my way with you, right?

CharcoalDreams: ~eep~ something like that. Okay, pretty much exactly like that.

InvaderZ: Keep that in mind as you turn that toy on and slide it slowly inside you. Imagine that's me. That first slow penetration. The slow build-up.

CharcoalDreams: Um, wow, okay. This is better than any fantasy I've ever come up with. Are you taking your time, almost pulling out of me before pushing back inside again?

InvaderZ: I am, but I don't know how long I can be patient.

CharcoalDreams: So make me come. Slam into me

hard and fast while you hold me in place. Listen to me get louder with each thrust.

InvaderZ: Fuck. I'm stroking myself really fast now.

CharcoalDreams: I'm moving my vibrator higher, pressing it against my clit. This feels so incredible. It should be you instead, sliding along my slit, listening to me moan…

InvaderZ:

CharcoalDreams:

InvaderZ:

CharcoalDreams:

InvaderZ:

CharcoalDreams: ~laughs~ Wow. I just came really hard.

InvaderZ: Holy fuck, that was incredible.

CharcoalDreams: Mmm…definitely. And I owe you an apology.

InvaderZ: Oh?

CharcoalDreams: I should have let you into my fantasies a long time ago.

InvaderZ: Nice. This doesn't get awkward now, does it?

CharcoalDreams: Only if you tell me we can't ever do it again ;-)

InvaderZ: Right. Who else is going to keep my hand and brain well lubricated for the next couple years?

CharcoalDreams: You say the sweetest things.

InvaderZ: Riley?

CharcoalDreams: Hmm?

InvaderZ: Thank you.

CharcoalDreams: ~Blush~

InvaderZ: I have to bolt. I'll message you next time I have a connection.

CharcoalDreams: I'll be here.

chapter one

Car exhaust and espresso. It smelled so wrong, but for Zane, it was almost perfect. Only one thing was missing. He scanned the cars passing the wooden shack, which was barely big enough for a coffeemaker and a couple of employees. *Where's Riley?*

It was April, too early in the year for many people to be occupying the plastic benches surrounding the drive-up coffee shop. He grabbed their drinks from the barista, knowing what kind of coffee she'd want, and picked one of the empty tables to set the cups down on.

He tapped his toes inside his shoes in time with the passing seconds. Why was he so on edge? Aside from the obvious *my past haunts my every waking and sleeping moment.*

Was he really nervous about seeing Riley again? Okay, so he'd been deployed in the Air Force for the past six years, but they'd kept in touch. Email, hanging out when he was on leave, and chatting online whenever possible.

Oh, and those chats. Heat flooded his veins at the rush of pleasant memories. *Chatting* was a bit of an understatement. He'd barely been gone for a year when their conversations changed. Got more intimate.

Jesus. The things they'd said to each other, wrapped in excuses like *we're thousands of miles apart* and *it's just two friends helping each other out.* For the sake of their friendship he hoped those conversations wouldn't come between them now, but that didn't stop his fantasies from running rampant with images of stripping her down. Pinning her against the wall. Making her scream with pleasure…

He shook the vivid thoughts aside. The last thing he wanted was for this to cause a gaping rift between them when they were face to face.

His pocket vibrated and he reached for his phone. Was she canceling? He wasn't sure if that would be a relief or a disappointment. When he saw the messages, he rolled his eyes, his irritation surging. They weren't from Riley.

Checking in.

How's civilian life?

I'm in your part of the country. Meet me for coffee?

He glared at the phone. No matter how many times he told Sabrina he wasn't interested, she kept trying to recruit him.

And now the memories of his deployment were back, along with emotions he'd rather not have. Guilt. Horror. Resignation. The thoughts tightened in his chest and danced in front of his eyes.

"Sexy love letters from your girlfriend?"

Riley's voice came from behind and jolted him back to the now. She wrapped her arms around his neck, her slender frame pressing into his back when she hugged him. She was almost as tall as he was, but experience told him she had to stand on tip-toe to do that. The familiar scent of cherry lip-gloss mingled with everything else and made it easier to stash his sins behind thoughts of her. Her breasts molded to him and rested against his shoulder blades.

He smiled and concentrated on falling into the sensations of her. "Hey, stranger."

"Hey, yourself." Riley settled her forehead against his shoulder. "Am I interrupting?"

It was easy to relax against her, as though with Riley's touch, the last six years faded. He pocketed his phone. He could tell Sabrina *no* for the fiftieth time later.

Zane spun to face Riley. "Not interrupting at all," he said. "I'm here for you." He couldn't stop from tracing his gaze over her. Fuck, was he here for her. Her long-sleeved T-shirt hugged round breasts, and her blonde hair framed a pixie-like face and a teasing smile. "How have you been?"

"Not nearly as great as I am right now." She locked her gaze on his, eyes bright blue and dancing with mischief. "I can't believe you're really back. For good. We have so much to catch up on. So much to do."

His sex-starved imagination seized and taunted him with the concept of what they could be doing. When he pushed aside the mental images of tasting her cherry-flavored lips, they left an empty spot for a new tension to dive in. A pang clattered in his gut, bringing memories of what he'd left behind in the Air Force.

That was one bit of *catching up on* that could wait until later. Or never. She didn't need that kind of burden. He swallowed the response, not letting it show on his face. "What have you been up to?"

"This and that." She turned her attention to the ground, fingers flying to the silver heart resting at the base of her throat. She still had the locked he'd given her in high school. The *Friends Forever* one.

The realization warmed him. "That's specific."

"Is this for me?" She grabbed one of the cups from the table.

"Only if you still like caramel lattes."

"Only if you need air to breathe." She kissed him on the cheek, took a long drink, and then dropped onto the bench across from him, fiddling with the paper sleeve on the cup.

Apparently, he wasn't the only one with secrets. "The last few years have been so good you don't even want to talk about them?"

She met his gaze. "Wrong." Her voice was a combination of finality and teasing. "You're the one who dropped off the radar two years ago. You don't get to waltz back into town as if you were never gone, and interrogate me about my life without giving me details in return."

He really wanted to avoid this conversation. But he could redirect if needed. "What do you want to know?"

"Where are you staying?"

He could answer that question. "One of Archer's spare rooms. He's letting me have it cheap, until I find work."

Riley's expression shifted in an instant, as her

furrowed brow melted into wide-eyed realization. "Really? And you're still wondering what I was up to?"

"Yes."

She gave a short laugh, but she didn't sound amused. "I'm kind of surprised he didn't mention it is all. We... Um... I was staying there for a while too."

That explained a lot. Riley and Archer, his two best friends, had a perpetual on-again, off-again relationship. "I thought you two were done." Funny how Archer didn't mention the on-again part of things when Zane mentioned where he was going this afternoon.

"We are, this time."

He'd heard that before. He raised an eyebrow.

"This is different from any other time," she protested. "Now. I answered your question. You answer mine. Give and take, right? Where did you go?"

Technically, nowhere. In truth, everywhere he hadn't wanted to. "Afghanistan. Iran. North Korea. You already know that." Her comment back then, when he gave her the basic details of his job, was *I always thought Air Force equaled being some hotshot, flying fighter jets. You really get to hone your hacking skills instead?* He'd told her it was called *intelligence.* Someone had to keep those hotshots safe in the air.

He should have stuck to doing exactly that. Guilt tried to worm its way back in, and he scrubbed it out. This gnawing shadow was going to be status quo for a while, wasn't it?

She clucked. "All of that happened before you dropped off the radar. Where have you been for the last two years?"

"How's the drawing coming?" He snatched the first topic he could think of. Riley was a brilliant artist. She kept saying she wanted to go pro. Step up and teach at the community college at least. Maybe try to publish one of her graphic novels.

While he was deployed, he'd happily sent her photos for reference shots—of him, of his Air Force buddies, all of it. Anything to help her with her passion.

"It's good. Now that you're back, you and your truck can model for me in person." She twirled her cup on the table. Her expression said she wasn't buying any of his attempts to change the subject. But she was letting him do it anyway.

"You drew my truck into your story?" It was an older model BMW 1602 he and Granddad converted into a truck when he was a teenager.

A hint of a smile crept back in. "It's got character. I love your truck. Your granddad let me take pictures whenever he pulled it out of storage for maintenance."

That made sense. Granddad adored Riley.

Silence fell between them. Their conversations had never been stilted, so why did the silence feel wrong, now? Because he was keeping secrets, and so was she. Why did she have to hook up with Archer? Again.

Not that Zane deserved a say in who Riley dated… And they never made him take sides, but it still made things awkward. "What else have you been up to?" he asked.

She clenched her jaw for the briefest of moments before her playful smirk returned. "There's not a lot to tell. Kenzie landed herself a sexy rich guy—you got a wedding announcement, right?—so I took over her condo payments. I'm thinking about buying it."

Which sounded fantastic, except for one teensy, tiny thing. "You hate living alone."

"I'm a big girl now. I can handle the scary noises. Speaking of..." She fiddled with her keys for a moment, before she finally pulled one from the ring. She leaned over the table and dropped the single key into his shirt pocket. "You're always welcome to stop by. It might be more comfortable hanging out at my place."

His cock stirred, and a desire seared over him when she glided her hands over his chest, and the way she bent at the waist gave him a fantastic view down the front of her shirt. Oh, so many shared fantasies.

She dropped back into her seat, toying with her hair, her gaze flitting everywhere. That felt out of place. It was like a dim image of what he remembered, but someone had missed something in the forgery. Her subtle discomfort didn't sit well with him. "Aren't you and Archer talking?"

Most couples that broke up tended to not speak, but Riley and Archer were different. They always made up when they weren't involved.

She turned her attention back to her drink. "We're working on it. It's still awkward, but friendship first. Right?"

"Always." Zane wouldn't overthink her question. Wouldn't wonder if she was talking about Archer, or about what she and Zane got up to.

This was why Riley never wanted to date Zane. She couldn't handle their friendship fracturing the way hers had with Archer. No one knew her better than Zane. She was so glad to have him back, she wasn't giving him up again.

Except this wasn't the Zane she hung out with years ago. The difference wasn't distinct, but he seemed more formal around her. Less at ease. And instinct told her it wasn't only because of the Archer mistake.

Please don't let it be the cybersex. The last thing she needed was to drive away her best friend because their online conversation got a little—or a lot—intense. Maybe once they got comfortable with each other again, it wouldn't be a big deal.

She and Zane had flirted since before they were old enough to realize they were doing it, and once upon a time, she thought he'd be her Prince Charming. She figured out years ago their relationship didn't work that way. He was the one man she felt comfortable saying that about. She could tease him all she wanted, and he gave as good as he got, but it didn't mean anything romantic.

"Does this whole *friendship first* thing mean I've lost my chance?" Zane stuck out his lower lip in an exaggerated pout, teasing dancing in his pale eyes.

As if. She laughed and shook her head. "Even if you didn't mean too much to me to just be some random hookup, I'm trying to change. I'm done falling for every guy who smiles at me."

"So, what? You're never dating again? Things might get a little lonely in the bedroom… You sure you can hold out?" Of course he had to go there.

Not that she minded the playful banter. This was so much better than sidestepping conversational landmines. "I've got a good vibrator. I've also got a lot better grasp on my desires than you and your so-called *celibacy*. We both know how not true that is."

His tiny smirk defied his attempt to look innocent. "I don't know what you're talking about. I haven't been with anyone since— Well, you know."

And… moment ruined. He meant Sabrina, the Air Force girlfriend. She still didn't know why he thought sleeping with a superior officer was a good idea. Riley studied him—the sturdy set of his jaw, the scruff of probably two days' worth of beard. *God,* he was sexy. "I didn't mean physically."

"Ah. Right." The corner of his mouth quirked up in a half-grin.

Riley was referring to all the times one of them had been lonely or horny, and their conversations became more than casual banter. "I'm guessing it's easier to hold out when you've got someone on call who you can talk dirty to."

"If you're saying that to cite my lack of willpower, I wasn't always the one asking."

"Whatever. Now that you're back, the tail is going to be throwing itself at you. You won't need me anymore." It was supposed to be a teasing comment. Tossed out without meaning. But the words tasted sour in the back of Riley's throat.

"I will always and forever need you."

His reassurance burrowed deeper than she expected, reassuring and soothing nerves she hadn't realized was exposed. "Me too. I mean—"

"I know what you mean."

Of course he did. That was part of who they were. And now they could get back to normal. No worries.

chapter two

"What happened with you and Archer?" Zane asked.

And they were back to that. Riley's neck tensed until it ached in her skull.

The Archer thing wasn't really a big deal. So why was she making it one? "Why do you think it was anything different than any other time?"

"Probably because you said this time was different. Also, because you won't give me a direct answer."

Riley fiddled with the locket hanging around her neck, tracing her thumb over the *Friends Forever* etched on the back. Zane wouldn't make fun of her if she told him. But she still questioned whether she'd done the right thing. "It maybe, possibly, didn't end on the best of notes."

"I got that much. What did he do?"

"He proposed."

"Proposed… a threesome? New bathroom towels?"

Seconds ticked away. She stared back. *Please get it. And please don't think I was stupid about it.* A sharp chill whipped through the afternoon, and she shivered and pulled her arms tight around herself. The April sun in Salt Lake City might be nice, but the moment it dipped behind the mountains, the cold sank in. At the drive-thru, someone's fan belt squealed. Children's voices carried from an open car window.

Zane's eyes grew wide. "Like down on one knee?" At least he didn't look disappointed—that was something to be grateful for—but she hoped for some kind of sign he wasn't going to hold it against her for walking away from something like that.

"Candlelit dinner, champagne—the works."

"And?"

"And I turned him down, and we decided maybe it was time we went our separate ways."

"I'm… sorry it didn't work out?"

That lacked sincerity. Relief trickled inside Riley. "No, you're not."

"I'm sorry it has you on edge. I wish I knew what the big deal was."

She twisted her mouth in frustration. Not with him, but with herself. "Everyone already thinks I'm a flake who can't maintain a solid relationship. Like… everyone. My sister. You—"

"I don't think that." He rested a hand on hers.

Warmth spread through her at the gentle touch. "Right. All this *what happened now* and *something always happens* stuff, and you don't think I'm a flake."

He dropped her hand but didn't pull back. "That's not about you. It's about Archer. The two of you aren't the same people around each other."

She ducked her head, guilt adding to her

lingering doubt. She didn't want to be the wedge in his friendship with Archer. Why couldn't she take Zane's explanation at face-value? "It's just that I had someone stable, with a good job, who didn't expect me to buy his weed or ask me if I wanted to do my twin sister while he watched, and what did I do? Told him *no* and walked away. Destroyed everything. Maybe my only chance at something good."

Zane clenched his hands into fists, his jaw growing tighter with each word she said.

Please don't let him close off again.

"I bet he didn't even get you the right ring." A smile broke through his shifting expressions.

She paused, brain wrapping itself around the words. Was he really talking about…? There was no way he remembered that. "It had a diamond on it. Solitaire, pretty, princess cut. You know, every girl's dream ring."

"Except yours."

It had been over a decade, and Zane still remembered. The realization warmed her. They'd been at the mall, and they passed a jeweler. She pointed out an engagement setting in the window and said, if she ever got married, she wanted something just like that. Low profile, so it didn't snag on anything, but brilliant and unique. She'd never seen anything like it before or since.

Back then, Zane made a face, said he didn't understand why girls spent so much time thinking about things like that, and then tugged her toward the food court.

"No. He didn't get me the right ring." She tucked a loose strand of hair behind her ear.

"Did you love Archer? *Do* you love him?"

She'd lost count of the number of times she asked herself that question, and she didn't know the answer. "He's a good guy."

Except for every habit he had that drove them apart. And those she had, which he hated. And that no matter how many times she tried to talk to him about it, he'd been boring in bed. And he thought her art was a waste of time. And… And… And…

But he'd never hit her or asked her for money. And he would have taken care of her.

Zane tugged at her fingers to draw her attention. "It doesn't mean the two of you belong together. Do you love him?"

It wasn't as if she knew what love really was. What if she did love Archer and was too dense to recognize it? "You're the only other guy I've ever met who's that considerate and fun. Okay, you're a billion times more those things, but you're also not the one who proposed."

"You're avoiding my question. If you prefer, if those are your only qualifiers for what makes marriage material, and supposedly I have them in spades, would you say *yes* simply because I asked?"

Her breath caught. Would she? The thought of Zane down on one knee, or even better, of her spending the rest of her life with him made her pulse race.

No. Romance ruined friendships. "No. I don't love him."

"So you made the right choice." He caressed her knuckles with his thumb.

She smiled, the reassurance not chasing away

her misgivings, but making it easier to believe she'd been right to walk away.

"You didn't answer my other question." He smirked and slid from his seat to come around to her side of the table. He dropped to one knee next to her and took her hand in his.

What's he doing? He's teasing me, right? Blood rushed in her ears, making it hard to hear. They'd been catching up for all of half an hour, and he was talking about love and marriage?

"Riley Ann Carter"—he locked his gaze on hers—"we've known each other forever."

Oh God, he's really doing this.

"You're the sexiest, most intelligent woman I've ever met."

Riley's heart stopped. He twitched. The corner of his mouth pulled up for the briefest moment.

He continued. "With your sister being a close second."

Her stomach plummeted. He was yanking her chain. Trying to distract her.

"Would you"—his serious expression faltered again—"and she make out, while I watch?"

Was that really relief flooding her or just the tiniest bit of hurt and disappointment? She smacked him on the arm. "You're an ass."

He sat on the bench next to her, his leg brushing her knee. "I'm sorry. I couldn't help it."

"You're not sorry."

"Promise me something?"

"What?"

"I meant what I said, except that last bit. You're the smartest, most fun and brilliant person I know.

Promise me, regardless of how many guys come and go, you won't marry one unless he deserves you—the amazing you—and that you'll never beat yourself up for turning someone down." He lifted her face with a finger under her chin. "Say it. Promise me."

"I promise."

"Want to get out of here?" Zane stood and offered her a hand up.

She shivered when another gust of wind rushed past her. Some place warmer might not be a bad idea. "Dinner?"

"I'm in. Where to?"

She let him pull her to her feet and landed closer to him than she intended to. The bite in the air stole her breath, and she let her attention linger on the heat of his grip. "You pick."

"I'm fine with whatever." The intensity of his gaze drilled into her in the most delicious way.

Her thoughts fuzzed, and all she could make sense of was the fading sunlight and the stillness around them. She didn't pull away, settling a hand on his chest instead.

His heart hammered under her palm. Maybe she needed to get back to the elephant in the coffee shop parking lot... "About what happened while you were gone."

"Which *what*?" His question was low and throaty.

Tingles rose under her skin from the way her body molded to his sturdy frame. "The flirting. The dirty talk. The long-distance mutual masturbation."

"What about it?" He placed his hand against the small of her back, holding her tight.

Heat flooded her, chasing away the chill in her legs. "Was it a mistake?"

"Do you think it was?"

No. God, no. That was what she wanted to say. What she'd wanted him to say.

She swallowed the response. As enticing as the thought of continuing things in person was, something ran underneath, tempering her desire. "It was fun, but we were both heartbroken and lonely. Besides, *in person* is a different story." Understatement of the century.

He dropped his arm from around her waist and stepped back. His shoulders relaxed, but the corners of his mouth tugged down. "It's true."

"I told you things I've never told anyone." She hadn't meant to admit that. "But having the expectation out there—"

"Exactly." He shoved his hands in his pockets. "It puts up a wall we don't want."

The conversation was rapidly deteriorating into a wall of its own. "So we're still friends, what was in the past is in the past, and we can move on?"

"No assumptions, no expectations. We don't have that kind of physical relationship."

The tension evaporated from her neck. "I appreciate that."

"Besides"—he relaxed—"I'd rather be friend-zoned than what you did to Archer."

Friend-zoned. She hated that phrase. It implied she owed someone sex because she was nice to them. "What happened to it not being my fault?"

He shrugged, his smile wilting. "I'm not saying you were wrong to turn him down; I completely agree. But you know… on again, off again. Giving him hope, when you know you don't love him."

She clenched her jaw. "If I'd known that, I wouldn't have given us another try. You know me better than that."

She thought he did, anyway. The reason she flitted from guy to guy was because she was looking for that special something. Love was such an elusive thing, she didn't want to miss out because she refused to look.

Zane crossed his arms. "It never works out. You destroyed that friendship a long time ago, and you keep trying with him. When you and Archer are together, he's this controlling, possessive jackass, and you keep going back to him anyway. It doesn't bother me that you're looking for something special, but you keep investing so much in these fucking losers. They're not right for you—it's obvious—and you still dive into it. It always ends with both of you miserable, and it wouldn't have to be that way if you recognized it from the start."

She narrowed her eyes. "I didn't realize you thought so little of me. So… what? This friendship is your version of pity for the girl who can't make up her mind because she's delusional about finding her Prince Charming? Or maybe you'd prefer I ran my choices by you first."

"That's not what I meant. I'm just saying you're too good for these guys. The same way I tell you every time you end up with another doorknob."

"Really?" She couldn't keep the hurt coursing through her from leaking into her reply. "Because it sounded like you were accusing me of being a heartless devourer of souls."

"You're being melodramatic."

"You're being a jerk." This was all wrong. It wasn't supposed to go this way. Six years apart, and they'd kept in touch... until two years ago. They'd remained friends while he had a psychotic fiancée. Now they'd been back together for less than an hour, and it was tearing them apart.

"Riley." He reached for her, but she pulled away. His frown deepened. "I didn't mean anything by it."

"Drop it. Don't make this worse."

"Please?" He grabbed her hand, holding her fingers between his. "You're this amazing, beautiful soul, and I get it—you see good in people who don't deserve it. It gets painful to watch sometimes."

That's what she got for dissecting her relationships with him online. A tiny voice whispered she was overreacting, and most of her agreed. That didn't stop Zane's words from digging deep, echoing with her own fears and insecurities. She swallowed it all, leaving a lingering bitter taste in her mouth. "I don't mean to do that to you. Dinner?"

"Yeah. All right."

The foot between them as they walked to his truck felt wider than the thousands of miles that had been there a week ago. Riley wanted to see this from his perspective. Most of her failed relationships were *meh* at best, but she wouldn't have known that if she'd walked away without giving them a chance.

Zane, though. If they could get past whatever this was, things could go back to right. She wouldn't let her mistakes bleed over into their friendship.

chapter three

Zane didn't know what to focus on first as he parked his truck on the street in front of the remodeled Victorian. Frustration? Hurt? Annoyance? Dinner conversation was stilted, and the meal had barely started before he and Riley both made their excuses to get back.

He never had to watch what he said around Riley before, but apparently things were different now.

He made his way up the sloping lawn to the storefront. Archer had inherited the house in The Aves from his grandmother. It had taken a lot of petitioning to get the city to license the project, but Archer finally got the permits to turn the main floor into a comic-book shop. The top floor was Archer's pad, and he'd converted the middle floor into two apartments, one of which was Zane's until he found a new source of income.

Work. The single word added another layer of dread to his dark mood and made his phone feel heavier in his pocket, weighing down his thoughts with the ignored text from Sabrina. A job offer.

Zane pushed into the store and snarled at the

chime that echoed through the open room. He made his way past rows of wooden backlog cases and metal shelves full of toys and the latest comic editions. He slid onto an empty stool, behind the glass counter, and waited, jaw clenched.

Archer was arguing with a brunette about whether or not the DC Comics reboot was a bad thing for the franchise. The words sounded like an argument anyway. Their smiles said it was anything but. She looked familiar. One of the five billion people Zane had met in the last day or so. Victoria, maybe?

"Your friend needs you more than I do." She gave Zane a smile. "His scowl will drive off customers."

"I'm fine."

"Right." She pushed a dress wrapped in a dry-cleaning bag toward Archer. "I'll be back later."

As she left, Zane leaned against a shelf. "She's cute."

Archer hung the dress—it looked like a Renaissance recreation made of velvet—on a nearby rack. "She's not Riley."

Fuck. There was the conversation opener he needed. "That's the point."

"I take it you didn't get a happy reunion." Archer turned, using the counter to mirror Zane's posture.

"Did you possibly forget to mention something?"

"I wouldn't say I forgot. As far as I know, she hasn't told anyone else. What makes you special?" Archer sighed. "Never mind. Forgot who I was talking to."

Zane rubbed his face. "What in the entire history of anything that has ever happened between the two of you made you think proposing was a good idea?"

"You vanished, and things between Riley and me were going better than before. I know she's got this vision of *happily ever after*. I figured maybe a ring was what was missing from the equation."

"Except the one thing that hasn't changed is she keeps dumping you."

"Yeah—well—I get it now, but that's not why you're pissed." Archer turned away at the sound of a chime, focusing his attention on the two teenagers who came in.

"Apparently more changed than I thought." Zane didn't want another fight.

"After all the time the two of you spent verbally jerking each other off, I'd figure things would be perfect between you." Sarcasm hung heavy in Archer's voice. "Or did one of you think that wouldn't change anything?"

Betrayal rocked inside Zane. "She told you about that?" So much for keeping it between them. What he and Riley had done was no-strings stress relief, but he hadn't expected her to think so little of it—and his friendship with Archer—that she'd… No.

Archer twisted his mouth. "Jen might have accidentally stumbled on an e-mail or two, when she was looking for something on Riley's laptop."

"You let your sister go through Riley's email?" Zane kept his disgusted tone low. Even if half their friends already knew, no reason to let the teenagers in the back of the store in on it, too. "And you wonder why the two of you never work out."

"You know what's made my life a whole lot happier?" Archer adjusted his position when the two teens disappeared behind one of the shelves. "Realizing Riley's all talk. She may be entertaining to hang out with, but she doesn't know what she wants out of life or the people around her, except that she wants it all to conform to her fantasy utopia."

Anger rushed through Zane. Archer had betrayed her trust, and was insulting her now? *Is he doing any worse than you did earlier?* Zane bristled at his mental question. "Really? You're blaming her for your inability to move on?"

"I've moved on." Archer tensed when the teenagers headed back toward the exit, one of them carrying a box with a bikini-clad figurine in it. "It's funny how, for someone who doesn't take sides, you always jump to her defense."

"Whatever." Zane pushed off the stool. A tiny part of him hoped the boys would bolt with the toy. Give him a justified confrontation. He couldn't ignore his disappointment when they set it on a shelf near the front door, before leaving.

The two kids paused halfway out, and turned to watch the woman walking in. If she noticed, she never flinched. She looked at Archer and grinned.

She was cute. Pixie-like face framed by short, dark hair that had a bright red streak running through it.

"Hey." Archer returned turned the smile. "How much of your stash do you want this week?" He let a lot of people pre-order things like special editions, but was generous about holding them until customers could pay. He had boxes under the counter and in the back room of comics and toys waiting for their unofficial layaway to end.

She stopped in front of the counter, and her gaze flicked to Zane, then a second time and her attention lingered. "I'll take it all."

"Does this mean you got the job? Am I wishing you farewell and best of luck?" Archer pulled a plastic bin from under the counter that held several books, and almost as many pieces of merchandise— a blanket, a T-shirt, a hat.

She glanced at each piece, but kept returning to look at Zane after. "Yes, and no. Atlanta wasn't in the stars for me, but I got my second choice and I'm staying here."

"Bummer, about Georgia. I know you really wanted the Skriddie position," Archer rang all the items up, and set them back in their crate.

Skriddie? Odd name for a company.

Mikki clacked a barbell tongue piercing against her teeth. Her boyfriend—girlfriend?—probably loved that. "Yeah, but nah. At least this way I don't have to find a new comic shop."

She handed Archer her credit card. Or tried to. She was watching Zane so closely, she jammed it into the register instead. She pulled back with a giggle, and adjusted her trajectory.

Archer shook his head. "Mikki, this is—"

"Zane Petrov," she said, extending her hand. "AKA, The Taurus. I'm such a huge fan."

"I have fans?" Zane didn't know how to react

to that. Especially when she addressed him by a screen name he didn't really brag about. Not these days, anyway.

Archer chuckled. "Mikki has an elite and unique list. Bill Gates, Steve Wozniak, Jared Tippins..."

Zane raised an eyebrow. How'd he make a list of tech's most notorious? "How do I hook up prospective employers with this passion of yours for... my work? What is it you think I did?" Since all of it was supposed to be classified. And none of it had been as The Taurus. His teenage hacking activities had landed him on one too many government watchlists, and he'd ditched the identity when he enlisted.

Mikki clacked her piercing against the top of her teeth. "Hacked Cord's servers. Released their game ahead of schedule. You're a legend."

"I don't exactly make that information public." Not that he could ignore the flush of pride that came from someone knowing. He'd done it in high school. To prove he could. It had been bragging rights when he was a teenager.

And impressed the fuck out of Riley. Her name flitted inside with ambivalence. They needed to find their center again.

"Like Archer said, I'm weird." Mikki ducked her head. When she looked up again, excitement shone in her eyes. "How'd you do it? Forced SQL injection string? Pulsing DDOS?"

"What is it you do?" Zane asked.

"Ethical hacking, for NetSafe Systems."

Zane wouldn't mind getting in on a job like that.

"Drop my name?"

"Are you serious?" Mikki's eyes grew wide. "Yeah, of course. Oh my god, that would be amazing to work with you. Give me your number."

Zane scribbled his information down on a scrap of paper.

"I'm still new." She tucked his phone number into a small pocket on her purse. "Duh. You probably guessed that. I don't have a lot of pull, but I'll tell my boss. Because seriously. Wow. You're just... I meant it, how did you do the Cord thing?"

Given her job, it probably wasn't impressive, but it had been top notch a decade ago. "I hopped a series of paths until I found the directory with the install files, and used a randomizer to guess the password. Network security wasn't the same back then."

"I want details. All the details." She glanced at her watch, and sighed. "But later." She grabbed one of Archer's business cards, scrawled on it, and handed it to Zane. "In case you want to follow the job stuff. Or go sing karaoke with me sometime, or get a drink... Whatever."

"Thanks." Zane stuffed her phone number into his wallet.

She grabbed her purchase, said her goodbyes, and was on her way.

"She's cute, right?" Archer asked when she was gone.

"Adorable. High energy. Seems smart." *She's not Riley.*

"Are you going to call her?"

Zane paused. He was on the other side of the

conversation he'd just had with Archer about Victoria. What was going on in his head? "I don't know. Maybe." But he wouldn't. Not like that.

"I'm gonna cut out for a while." Zane pushed away from the counter and headed upstairs. How badly did he fuck up tonight with Riley?

chapter four

Riley sank back in her chair. She'd been staying in her sister's condo for months, but it still didn't feel like home. It didn't help that most of the furniture was Kenzie's, and a lot of it was more for show than comfort. She squirmed on the wooden seat. Maybe it was time to get some better cushions for the Ethan Allen dining set.

She was trying to get some sketching done. It usually helped her relax, but now she couldn't focus. Every few seconds, she glanced at her phone. Zane had texted her a few times since their awkward reunion two nights ago. Generic *how are you,* and *job interview, wish me luck* stuff. Her replies were just as terse and empty. She wasn't sure what to say.

He'd only been back a few days, and they'd destroyed a lifetime of friendship. Or he was right about her being melodramatic.

She took a deep breath, to steady her shaking hand.

What do we need to do to move past the other night?

She set the phone back on the table and stared at it, willing it to give her good news. Still, she was startled when it vibrated against the polished oak a few seconds later, sending a loud hum through the condo.

I was a jackass. Give me another chance?

A whisper of relief trickled through her. *Always :-)*

I'm coming over.

She grinned. She wasn't sure how these few words felt more meaningful than every other note they'd passed in the last few days, but she wouldn't argue. She'd tease him a little, though. She replied, *You're assuming a lot.*

Yup. Give me fifteen minutes.

Already feeling infinitely better, she turned her attention back to her sketching. With the looming cloud of frustration gone, she sank into the lines and figures as they met and blended and became recognizable shapes.

When a knock rattled through the apartment, she jumped. She laughed at the empty room and pushed her sketchbook aside. She was on her feet in an instant to yank open the front door.

Zane stood on the other side, raking his fingers over his short black hair. He gave her a hopeful smile. "So I can bask in your presence again?"

Once upon a time, Zane's combination of self-effacing jokes and pretending to put her on a pedestal made her uneasy. She learned it was just words, though. His way of keeping things light.

"I suppose." She intertwined her fingers with his and tugged him toward the kitchen table. A warm tingle spread through her at the contact, and she let the touch linger longer than needed.

He dropped her hand the moment she loosened her grip. She bit back a frown. He'd never been as physical as her, but he'd also never pulled away from her before.

No big deal. They needed to find their comfort zone again. "Are you free for a few hours? You can stay and help me plot and just hang out."

"Sounds fantastic."

"Good, you can cheer me up." She flopped into her chair, relieved when he took the seat next to her instead of across the table. She winked.

"Are you okay? What happened?"

Apparently, she needed to tease harder. True, a random person would stare at her blankly for most of her incomplete comments. Things were different with Zane. Or at least, before he left, he would have gotten her. "I'm not seeing eye to eye with my best friend."

"We'll get there." A faint hesitation cut through his words.

Instead of overanalyzing the situation, she pushed her sketchpad toward him. "What do you think?"

He turned the pages. "I'd forgotten how amazing you are at this. I mean, I've always known you were good, but your talent still floors me."

"It's only a rough outline." Heat flooded her cheeks, and she ducked her head, even though he wasn't watching her.

"That makes it more amazing. Is this… This isn't me, is it?"

She followed his finger. "Technically, yes. I'm using photos of you to create him."

"You're sure?"

Had she done something wrong? Had the compliments been lip-service? "Why?"

"He's blond."

She rolled her eyes and tugged the sketchbook away. "It's not supposed to literally be you. You're just a point of reference." She liked to keep fantasy Zane all for herself. The one on the page had to be different.

He tilted his head, still studying the image, though it wasn't in front of him anymore. "You made him all wiry. Like skinny but muscular. How is that even possible?"

It was an exaggeration, based on the art style, but the form was one thing she knew she had right. She watched Zane, not successfully hiding her amusement.

He finally met her gaze. He finally looked up. "What?"

She made a show of raking her gaze over his defined chest and sturdy arms. His martial-arts training kept him in shape before he left, but his time in the Air Force had honed his form more. Too bad asking for nude shots—strictly for reference purposes, of course—wouldn't be appropriate. "You tell me. How do you pull it off?"

"Is this the one you're going to sell? Or is this for your portfolio, to get that teaching job? Both?"

Her amusement wavered, uncertainty sinking back in. Times like this she wished she'd never mentioned she wanted to do something professional with her art. It was a nice fantasy, but he'd grabbed the idea and clung to it, reminding her whenever he could that she needed to do it. It was the big reason he'd agreed to model for her. She suspected his reminders would become more frequent now he was back.

"I still have so much research to do."

He stared back, skepticism painting his expression. "Have you started?"

"I've poked around a little. I have a list of names to look into." She didn't want to have this conversation. It seemed like there were a lot of those between them now.

"We should go out." His too-cheerful announcement came from nowhere.

It was a great idea. So why was she hesitating to agree? "So we can stumble on more awkward topics we need to avoid?"

"So we can get past them."

She couldn't expect everything to be the same. They needed to adjust to who they'd become.

"All right." She pushed back from the table. "Give me ten minutes to wash this charcoal off and change into something less graphite covered."

"I'll be here."

Disappointment trickled through her, and she squashed it. Hoping he'd offer to help was the last thing she needed to do. Still, she couldn't shake the memory of his hand resting at the small of her back. The hammer of his heart against her palm. Maybe…

No. Bad. She wasn't going to consider what might have happened if he kissed her. If they'd stumbled back to his truck together. If he'd lifted her onto the tailgate and pushed between her legs. Or rather, she wouldn't consider it too much.

She tried to be quick about getting ready, hating to make anyone wait. Once the pencil residue was gone, she grabbed a fitted long-sleeved tee from her closet. She was pulling on her jeans when her cell phone rang in the other room. "Will you get that?" she called through the closed door.

"Yup."

She finished dressing, ran a brush through her hair, and yanked open her bedroom door. She came up short, breath caught in her throat when she almost ran into Zane.

He was less than six inches away. She needed to put some distance between them, but she couldn't get her feet to move.

He was close enough she felt his heat and smelled the crisp musk she always associated with him. She couldn't pull her gaze from his. What had they been doing before? She reached out and ran her fingers over the short black hair on top of his head. "I miss this being long."

He leaned into the touch, resting his hand on her hip. "It'll grow back."

"Hello?" A digitally muffled voice cut between them.

He held up her phone. "It's Kenzie."

Right. Reality. She took the phone from him, and put enough space between them to clear her thoughts. Sort of. "Thanks," she said again. "Hey, Sis."

Zane leaned against the far wall in the hallway, something unreadable in his gaze. Heat spread through her at his attention.

"Am I interrupting?" Kenzie's question was

lighthearted.

Riley couldn't help but wish they'd been doing something to interrupt. "I just got out of the shower." She winced when she realized how that sounded. "Alone."

Zane's mouth twitched with the threat of smile. She spun away to hide that the single gesture had eased her sour expression.

"As long as he hasn't moved in."

Riley sighed, making sure it was loud enough to echo through the receiver, but she didn't mind the teasing. Maybe now wasn't the best time to mention she'd given Zane a spare key. "You're not as funny as you think you are. What's up?"

"Grump. Have dinner with us next weekend. Both of you."

Riley wanted to keep up her stern demeanor, but she liked spending time with Kenzie and Scott. "All right. I'll be there, and I'll ask him."

"Fantastic. I'll let you two get back to whatever, and I'll e-mail you details."

They exchanged goodbyes, and Riley tucked the phone into her jeans' pocket. "Where to?" she asked Zane.

"Duh? That is, if it's still there."

She grinned. There was one place they always went. It was half-bar, half-arcade, and one of their favorite spots in the valley. "It definitely is."

"Epic." He didn't pull away when she intertwined her fingers with his and tugged him outside and toward the parking lot.

"I'm glad you knew what I was talking about. I had this flash of panic thinking everything I knew had changed, and the entire world had flipped upside-down." His tone was playful as he gestured wildly.

"Say I was a pod person. Would you really miss much about me?"

Only after they were both inside the truck—which smelled of coffee and Zane—did he say, "I'm not answering that."

"You brought it up."

He navigated traffic smoothly. "I know. I shouldn't have. Whenever I say stuff like that, it gets me in trouble. No one actually wants to know what you think of them, unless it's really good. They only think they do."

That made it sound like his opinion of her wasn't good. Now she had to know. Maybe he wasn't teasing after all? "I'm not them. If you don't tell me, I'll… um…" She'd what?

He glanced at her, one eyebrow raised, and then turned his attention back to the road. "Yes?"

Crap. She had no idea how to threaten him and still keep it light-hearted. "I'll pout?"

The truck stopped for a red light, and he shifted in his seat. He traced a finger over her protruding lower lip. "I don't know if that's a threat or a promise."

The contact sent a pleasant chill through her, and she parted her lips with a tiny gasp.

His gaze lingered on her face before he looked away. "That look though—that's worth spilling a lot of secrets for."

Geez. What would it take for him to do that again? Traces of his touch lingered, and his husky comment danced in her skull. Taunting her. Fire raced through her cheeks, and she pressed her forehead against the cool glass. The heat from the vents rushed over her skin. How big a deal would it be if she asked him to pull over and run that finger, or all of them, over more of her?

"I would miss everything about you." His soft comment startled her. "The way you reserve yourself and your judgment until you get to know someone. But you give everyone that chance. That not a lot of people know the real you and that you like to have a lot of fun."

His compliments didn't help redirect her thoughts. Instead, they enhanced the desire tingling on her lips. She turned back to him, studying his clenched jaw. The words rolled through her head, simple but surprisingly observant. "Not everyone thinks those are quality traits."

The corners of his mouth twitched. "Not everyone's opinion is worth listening to. Besides, since I'm one of the few you let in, I'm biased."

Giddiness rippled through her. She knew better than to fall hard and fast, and if she made that mistake with Zane, she'd lose one of the two most important people in her life. Only Kenzie mattered to her as much as he did.

This wasn't falling. She wasn't stupid. This was the same playfulness they'd always had. But she had a grander appreciation for it now.

This was friendship, nothing more. Even if her skin and her heart whimpered at the denial.

chapter five

Cheers for the series of games running on TVs around the room echoed in the background, dancing with the clank of mugs on tables and coins sliding into slots.

Zane nudged the plate and last slice of pizza in Riley's direction. He'd missed this—the less-than-healthy food, the mania of the crowds, all of it.

She pushed it back toward him with a smile and a shake of her head. "Not going to happen."

His, "Your loss," was muffled, as he took a large bite and then knocked back the last of his root beer in a single swallow.

She finished scribbling on the paper napkin and stuffed the pen back into the mini purse attached to her wrist. She slid the sketch across the table. "Something like that."

He studied the blue lines that made up the Chinese dragon. She'd drew it to give him an idea of something she was trying to explain, but he loved the artwork. God damn, she was incredible. "You never cease to amaze me."

"Thanks." Pink tinged her cheeks.

This wasn't a bad sight either. "Can I keep it?"

"Um…" She shrugged. "I guess. I was going to throw it out."

What a waste of stunning art. He folded the napkin before placing it in his wallet. "What next?"

The scents of oregano and beer filled the air with a comforting aroma. The stack of tokens that came with the meal sat on the table between them. They'd agreed food first, games second.

She swung her feet below the high seat, occasionally hooking them on the rungs before tugging loose again. "Pool?"

He'd known that was coming. Even if the case sitting next to her purse didn't have her custom cue in it, he could have guessed she'd pick pool. "Air hockey first," he said. It was as unfair as her suggestion, but since he'd relent eventually, his masculinity wouldn't suffer as much if he at least won at one thing before the night was over.

She screwed up her face, but laughter danced in her eyes. "All right."

He pocketed the tokens and led her toward the tables near the far end of the bar. The racket of pucks zooming back and forth clattered off walls and his eardrums. That wouldn't stop him from trying to carry on a conversation. The compressor under the table rumbled to life, and he grabbed his mallet before it vibrated out of reach. The smooth plastic was cool against his palm.

"So, six years in the Air Force, talk of going career, and suddenly you've been discharged. What happened?" She raised her voice when the puck started flying between them.

He faltered, and the puck slid into his goal. Of

course she was going to ask from a different angle. If it was an off-the-cuff question, he could give her a generic response and be off the hook. "Things change."

"That's definitive." She followed the movement of the plastic disc as it slid everywhere. "What kind of things?" The projectile bounced off her fingers, and she jerked her hand away. The puck rocketed around and found its way to her goal before she could recover.

"I got an offer from the CIA." Even though it was one of the last things he wanted to do. Memories and guilt assaulted him. He summoned a wall from deep inside and blocked off the emotions associated with that part of his past. Mostly. If he kept his response casual, maybe she'd move to another subject.

"Wait. What?" Riley watched, as the next six shots slid past her. Her attention wasn't on the game anymore. The table stopped rumbling with the finality of Zane's winning goal. She joined him on his side before he could ask for another round. "I thought you were looking for work," she said.

He should have known changing the subject wouldn't be that simple. He shrugged. "I turned them down." Discomfort churned inside, joined by regret and the phrase *not soon enough*. Even if part of him still considered going back. Calling Sabrina and telling her he was in after all. He jammed the doubts back down. They wandered the room until they stopped in front of a racing game with two plastic cars side by side.

She picked the red one. "Because they weren't

going to challenge you enough?"

Beyond paying the bills, he'd never been concerned about the size of his paycheck. From the time Zane was old enough to understand, Granddad had drilled home that someone only needed enough money for comfort. There was no need to be greedy, but the thought of doing any work that didn't make him think made Zane's skin crawl. Which, conveniently enough, meant Riley had given him his way out.

"Something like that." He dropped a couple tokens into the machine. The digital racetrack roared to life on screen, and the countdown to the start of the race began. He gripped the wheel in front of him and steered, leaning with each turn. The plastic car moved with him, though it didn't impact his driving onscreen.

"I get it. You could've just said *topic off limits*." Riley squealed as her car skidded around a tight turn, and he passed her. She corrected her direction onscreen and caught up, managing to pace his silver roadster. "Anyway. How'd the interview go yesterday?"

While his job hunt wasn't as unpleasant a topic as his military service, it was pretty high on his list of things he'd rather not dwell on. Mikki had gotten his foot in the door, but he hadn't been able to close the deal. Or even make it past the screening.

His car slowed and then stopped, and she left it in the dust, crossing the finish line third. The screen flashed, prompting them to insert another coin to continue.

He dropped his hands from the wheel. "Pool

next?" He couldn't put off the game forever, and it should get the lighter mood back.

"I'll go easy on you." She pulled a small tube from the purse dangling from her wrist and applied gloss.

He forced back the pulse that raced through him at the shine on her full lips and the hint of cherry in the air. "I'll be fine." His protest was weak as they walked toward the billiard tables. He'd never been able to figure out pool. Drunk off her ass and blindfolded, Riley could still whip him. She'd competed when she was in college. "I'm going to pretend I know what I'm doing and that you're just more pro than me," he said. The latter was true. Riley was more pro than most people.

"Whatever you have to tell yourself," she teased. She grabbed a couple of different cues, tested their weight, and then handed him one, before pulling hers from its case and piecing it together.

He fumbled to hold the stick right, but her cringe told him the impossible positions he kinked his fingers into weren't the right ones. She set her cue aside and covered his hand with hers. A pleasant warmth rushed through him at the contact. She positioned his grip in a more natural way. Her touch lingered, palm soft and inviting against the back of his hand.

"It was for ethical reasons." The admission slipped out before he could stop it. "Me turning down the CIA job."

"Oh." She dropped her hand and stepped away. "I think you've got it. Want to try taking a shot?"

"Not really. You show me how."

He shouldn't have said that. It was going to be tough enough to get things back to normal between them. Now a secret that really only needed to haunt him was trying to force its way out. She knew he'd been on the front line overseas, but for the most part, they never talked about the details. He tended to change the subject, and she never pushed.

She racked up the balls and set the cue ball a few feet back. The way she moved was flawless as she slid into the correct posture and lined up her angle. She knocked off her shot, and colored balls scattered across the table to bounce off rubber bumpers. Three of them slid into pockets.

At least he already expected her to kick his ass. It almost took the edge off. Zane snorted. "That was the equivalent of showing me a scribble next to a Rembrandt, then telling me to just add shading, to make one into the other." He dropped his stick on the table. "We should go back to the air hockey."

"You're overthinking it." She maneuvered next to him and put the cue back in his hand. "Relax, and just take your shot." She grabbed the white ball from where it had landed, inches from a pocket, and set it back in the center of the table.

She stood close enough he felt her heat and smelled the sharp tang of cherry. Desire prickled along his skin, spurred by her body and fantasies of licking along her skin. He bent at the waist, careful of how his semi-hard shaft met the edge of the table. "It's war, right? Things happen."

Great. She was within pin-her-to-the-wall-and-kiss-her-until-they-couldn't-breathe proximity, and he was talking about his demons. Rather than dwell on the past, he pushed the stick toward its target. The cue head bounced off the felt and jumped over the ball instead of hitting it.

"Try again."

He sighed and repositioned himself. "Maybe I shouldn't have been so picky about the job. I don't have any actual qualifications to do what I do. Not like real-world experience." The words tasted foul. What the fuck was his problem?

"Because what you did doesn't count as experience? I mean, I know you can't give me specifics, but to keep you interested for so long, it had to be intense."

Intense. That was one way to put it. He'd tried to make the same point to the interviewer. Sort of. "That's the problem. Since I can't go into detail… They say, *tell me about a time you solved a really big problem that saved an employer money.* I can't tell them what I really did, so what comes out is, *I did some stuff with computers, and it was really high-end, I promise.* Yeah, that's convincing."

He held up the cue in frustration. "Are you going to show me how to do this right, or not?"

"Fine." She let out a mock sigh. Moving next to him again, she positioned his left hand properly. She settled her right arm against his and rested her chest against his back. She pressed her cheek against his bicep, helping him line up the cue. "I'd go on about angle and trajectory and all that, but for me it's instinct." She pulled back his arm and helped him take the shot.

The balls scattered again, and three more slid into pockets. He had no idea what he'd just done. All he knew was how incredible she felt pressed against him. He dropped the cue but didn't pull away.

"You've gotten better," she said

"I tried to get a little practice in." His hand settled under hers.

He should move. Put some distance between them. Her heat seeped into all his senses, pushing past frustration and demons and awkwardness, and driving straight to his dick. *Fuck.* Riley had always been touchy-feely, but this pushed buttons he never realized he had.

He wanted her. He wanted to strip her down right here and make their dirty talk a reality.

And the last thing he wanted to do was hurt her. A little pain was all right, but heartbreak…

In a single motion, he twisted from her touch, spun, and grabbed her wrists before she could pull away. She locked her gaze on his—eyes wide and shocking blue. When she licked her bottom lip, any words he had evaporated, lost in his desire to dip in and taste her.

"What's wrong?" Though her question was soft, it stood out among all the background noise. Distinct and tempting.

The few faint snatches of reason left in his head pointed out he didn't want to go down this road with Riley. She deserved better than a hard-on-fueled fuck-fest in the back of his truck. She deserved better than him.

He dragged the reminder to the front of his thoughts and forced his voice to remain firm. "I know we said the what happened while I was gone is done and over—the past is in the past, sex ruins friendships, all that—so fair warning. You're way too tempting to ignore when you do things like press your body against me."

That should have been that. He expected her to pull away, maybe refuse to look him in the eye, and then they'd find a new comfortable middle ground.

Instead, she shifted her weight, rubbing her frame against him. "You say that like it's a bad thing."

Fuck, fuck, fuck.

"It is if you meant what you said." There was no way she didn't feel how hard he was, his cock digging into her hip. Impulse surged stronger. The one that wanted to bend her over the pool table, regardless of how crowded the place was, and drive inside her.

She didn't struggle against his grip, even when it tightened enough for his fingers to dig into her skin. A flush spread over her face, and her pupils dilated. "Do you really think the cyber stuff was a mistake?"

He swallowed. How the hell was he supposed to answer that? "I never said that."

"You implied it."

He forced the gears in his brain to unstick—to push past her soft scent, her gentle curves, her skin against his. "Neither one of us wants to get attached," he said.

"I never said anything about getting attached." The corner of her mouth pulled up in a mischievous smile, and she broke one hand away from him. She trailed down the chain around his neck, grasped his dog tags, and tugged lightly.

"You don't want to go down this road." His restraint had stretched past its snapping point. He gripped her wrist. Hard.

Her delighted gasp didn't help. "I do. Tell me you're not interested, and I'll never mention it again. No hard feelings." Her lips hovered centimeters from his, obliterating reason.

Pinning her down. Running his hands over her body. Experiencing in person the moans that drove him wild over the phone. If she were involved in a no-strings non-relationship with him, maybe she'd think harder about falling for the next doorknob that came along.

Logic argued that didn't make sense.

He gagged logic and shoved it in a closet. "What about sex ruining friendship?" It hadn't yet. Even if they hadn't gotten physical, they'd described about everything else to each other.

She hesitated, but her confidence flooded back quickly. "I promise it's just sex, and so do you. I trust you, so if you say it, I'll believe you."

Seemingly from nowhere, someone collided with Riley, and beer spilled over her top. Zane let go as she gasped and jerked back, her hands flying up. The booze soaked her pale shirt, suctioning it to her body so it clung to every curve. Zane struggled to pull his gaze from her tight form, full breasts, and rigid nipples, visible through the lace of her bra.

"Watch where you're going." A large man stood next to them. He slammed a mostly empty beer stein on the pool table, dribbles running over his clenched fist.

Fury nudged Zane's senses. Loudmouth ran into her, not the other way around.

Riley flinched away, brow furrowed. "What the

hell?" She shook her hands, and drops of beer splattered the floor around her.

"Stupid bitch."

Anger spurred Zane forward, powered by protective instinct, and unrequited lust. In an instant, he was nose-to-nose with the loud asshole. "Apologize."

"Fuck you." Loudmouth pushed Zane's shoulder. The stench of warm beer radiated from him. "Tell your bitch to watch where she's going."

All conversation stopped around them. People turned to stare, and camera phones came out.

"It's okay. It's not a big deal." Riley's pleading voice was soft amid the growing murmurs.

Zane didn't like fighting, but there were some things a person just didn't back down from. Like seeing his friend blamed by a drunken jackass for something she didn't do.

He grabbed Loudmouth's wrist and pulled it away from his own shoulder. In a single movement, he twisted and was behind Loudmouth, pulling the other man's fingers toward the base of his neck. Zane applied enough pressure to convey he could do worse, but not enough to cause injury. "It is a big deal. He owes you a new shirt, but a genuine *I'm sorry* would be a good start."

Loudmouth growled and jerked away, breaking Zane's grip on him. "Fucking asshole. I'm sorry your stupid girlfriend got in the way of my beer." He tensed his shoulders, spread his feet shoulder-width apart, and brought his fists up in a boxing stance. He wavered in his stance before steadying himself.

Zane kept his posture casual, staring back

without flinching. If Loudmouth lunged, he'd find himself on the ground with a mouthful of carpet, and probably a broken bone or two. Zane only partly hoped it would come to that. He made sure the anxiety of his hammering heart didn't show in his movements. The seconds ticked away, seeming to stretch into eternity.

"Asshole." Loudmouth narrowed his eyes for a moment, and then turned toward the exit, grumbling under his breath.

There was no need for Zane to go after the guy. All he wanted to do was diffuse the situation. As his adrenaline receded, the reassurance repeated in his head until he almost believed it.

"Excuse me." A firm voice jarred Zane from his brief meditation. "I'm going to have to ask you to leave."

Zane eyed the bar employee, the *fight* part of *fight or flight* still coursing through him. The guy was shorter by a couple of inches but bulkier, and the way his shirt stretched over his chest said he was muscular. Zane swallowed the resurge of instinct. He'd already dispatched the threat.

He shook his head, to clear out any residual argument, and wrapped an arm around Riley's waist. "Right. Sorry about the floor." He tossed a five on the table before leading her outside.

Almost every gaze in the room followed their short path. The stench of greasy food and booze threatened to resummon Zane's dinner. Maybe he shouldn't have had that last slice of pizza. They pushed outside, and the cool air washed over them.

chapter six

Riley should be embarrassed about what happened inside with the drunken asshole, or upset about being asked to leave or something. Instead, all she could focus on was whether or not she'd made a mistake suggesting no-strings sex with Zane.

Her thoughts were still stuck on his cock digging into her, moments earlier. The dampness that pooled between her legs when he grabbed her wrists. Her desperate desire to find out how he kissed.

Zane opened the passenger door of his truck and reached behind the seat. He grabbed a spare T-shirt and handed it to her. "I should take you home."

The dismissal nagged her. She had to resurrect this somehow. He was as interested as she was. If she could change out of her ruined top here, she didn't need to go home. She dropped into the passenger seat. "Don't move."

She reached behind her back to unclasp her bra, and his eyes grew wide.

"Do you want me to turn around?" he asked.

The flush was sexy, and the propriety was endearing. If he hadn't already turned away, maybe he was still considering what she'd said. She let out a tiny laugh, trying for seductive but—she was pretty sure—coming off as nervous instead. "I said, don't move. You're my human curtain."

In a single fluid gesture, she managed to pull off her soaked shirt and bra and slip the new one on without completely exposing herself. As she poked her head through the top of the shirt, she caught a glimpse of him forcing his gaze from her chest back to her face.

"That takes talent." His voice was an octave lower. She knew that sound. She'd heard it a few times on the phone, when he told her how he wanted to tie her to the bed and fuck her till she screamed.

And now that image was in her head. She ducked her head, feigning shyness. "Thank you for what you did in there."

He leaned against the frame of the truck, studying her. She couldn't read the thoughts behind his eyes, but she could almost convince herself the worst thing she saw was uncertainty.

"Does this mean you don't need to go home and change after all?"

So she hadn't completely ruined things. Relief flooded her. "Not yet. Did you have something in mind?"

"Let's drive and talk."

He closed her door, and seconds later, he was seated and pulling onto the road. But he wasn't talking. His gaze stayed fixed on the road, his hands on the steering wheel.

Riley shifted in her seat. What should she say? She hadn't planned to proposition him, but as the night wore on, the idea had climbed into her head and refused to budge. And when he all but laid out that ultimatum, she had to grab her chance.

Sure she was done with falling in love, and the best way to break the habit was to stay single. But Zane was right that she really missed the sex that typically came with being half a couple. More than six months without a guy to cuddle up against, clothed or otherwise, left her with a longing that her toys didn't sate.

And more than two years of no contact with Zane, after everything, made her body plead for him to be the solution.

Besides, he wasn't looking for commitment either. They already knew so much about each other. She adored him, but not romantically. There was no one else, except may be her sister, she trusted more.

She watched the road fade into the darkness as his truck climbed farther away from the houses dotting the side of the mountain. They were on the east side of the valley, high above even the multi-million-dollar homes. The valley floor with its endless lights made the sky and its stars look like a reflection.

They pulled onto the shoulder of a familiar dirt road. Riley didn't know how many nights they'd spent on the side of the mountain, either wanting a view of the fireworks shows below or just talking.

He shut off the engine and stared ahead, gripping the steering wheel. He finally turned to her. Something heavy and sad lingered behind his pale eyes. His smile was weak. "I hope this is okay."

"Of course." Her fast reply sounded too loud—

too chipper—to her ears.

He climbed out. "You coming?"

God I hope so. Maybe best to keep that thought to herself for now.

She followed him to the back of the pickup. He dropped the tailgate and slid into the bed, back to the wall, one knee pulled up to his chest, and arm resting on top.

She hid her frown. His posture wasn't a good sign. There had been a time when they'd have lain down in the back of the truck to watch the stars, her head on his shoulder, and never thought anything of it. Now he looked as though he didn't want her anywhere near him.

They could talk through this. It would have been nice if he'd agreed to take things to the next level, but she'd said *no hurt feelings* if he wasn't interested. She crawled into the truck bed opposite him and leaned forward, legs tucked to the side.

"So, not that it's a big deal…" he said.

Oh geez, she really had screwed up. "You know it sounds like a very big deal, right?"

"I do." He dropped his forehead onto his knee for a moment before looking at her again. "You wanted to know where I'd been for the last two years."

Her breath caught, and her pulse slowed. Desire skittered away in favor of hearing whatever he needed to say. "I figure it's *top secret*, but I am curious."

He gave a bitter laugh. "*Top secret.* Yeah."

"Tell me what you're allowed. I'm listening."

"A couple of years ago, I got a new assignment.

They wanted me doing some heavier surveillance. It was a huge challenge, so I jumped on it."

Of course he did. If his tone weren't so somber, she would have smiled.

"They told me I was getting them into some really tough places. Networks most people couldn't crack. Then they gave me someone new to report to."

"Okay…?"

He ran his fingers over the stubble on his head. "We did this differently than I'd ever done surveillance before. This woman excelled at her half of the job, and the entire idea was brilliant. Terrifying, but brilliant."

Riley forced back her wince at the unabashed compliment for another woman. "How so?"

"You know how phishing and spoofing work, right?"

She nodded. The recipient clicked on a link they thought was taking them to one place, and it took them to another instead, while capturing the associated login information.

"This is spoofing meets psy-ops. She chatted people up online. Nothing damning. Friendly shit—*How's the dog? Did you have a good vacation?* If she couldn't connect with her target online, she'd do it in person. Pose as a waitress, barista, or random lady at the gym. Whatever. The goal was never to dig deep. She only wanted to talk about the kind of things most people let slip to the right stranger. That work is stressful, or their back hurts, or the kids kept them up all night worrying about college admissions."

It sounded so benign. Which cranked Riley's

curiosity.

"My job…" He paused. "My job was to send those people email. Spoof it and make it look like it was from someone they knew and trusted. A boss. A girlfriend. A daughter. I had to make the email completely real and passable, so it didn't get stuck in some spam filter. The recipient clicked the link—I don't know, social media, whatever—and it passed through a gateway that downloaded the tiniest little Trojan in history, and we had full access to their computer. They ended up where they thought they were going and never questioned it."

"Wow." She was wary enough not to click those stupid links from strangers that said things like, *guess what I just heard about you online*, but never hesitated when the messages from her friends looked genuine.

"Yeah." He dragged out the word. "It wasn't my job to look where we were going, just to get us there and make sure we stayed."

Riley's head spun with the information.

"Except one night, things changed." Zane traced tight lines around a bolt in the tuck bed.

"What?"

"She left me alone for the first time."

"Before that, you were together twenty-four, seven? Long stakeout?"

He let out a dry laugh. "Something like that. I only figured out later, but it had a lot more to do with the fact that I wasn't under the same watch restrictions as before."

"Watch restrictions?" This was some straight-out-of-the-movies shit.

He nodded. "I poked harder than normal that night. I got bored and skimmed one of the computers I'd planted the back door on. The name caught my attention. American name. American IP… There was absolutely nothing top secret about that machine. It was some teenager's laptop. The worst things on it were a couple of emails she'd sent a friend, about sneaking out to get drunk that Friday night."

"Why were you spying on American teenagers?"

"I wondered that too. Every time my CO left me alone after that, I dug into another machine. The further I went, the more I looked, the more I realized I wasn't fighting the war I signed up for.

"This was some serious CIA shit. We were spying on civilians. The kind of people no one realizes are a threat to national security. Some of it was monitoring for treason-level shit, like ensuring no one was selling our secrets. Most of it was more benign—ensuring there was no price fixing on contract bids. Things along those lines."

She didn't know what to say. It was so Tom Clancy, but digital with a heavy side of invasion of privacy. "How does knowing someone's teenager got drunk on Friday night tell you if they're selling out their country?"

"No one is tight-lipped every hour of every day. Especially not the people who think they're too smart to get caught. Some senior VP for a military contractor finds a second source of income from a country who may not be so fond of us, or he takes a bribe during contract negotiation—anything like that. He keeps his mouth shut in public, but he usually tells his wife. Even if he doesn't, suddenly the family has things they didn't before. The kids are going to expensive private schools, or they're bragging to their friends about the new swimming pool, or the wife has a new car. A new wardrobe."

That made a scary amount of sense. "So you looked for anomalies."

"*I* didn't, but I made it possible for someone else to." He shook his head, doubt and anger hiding behind his gaze. "As I dug some more, I realized she—my new commanding officer—was on location with me, to try to make my job change to the CIA official. Which made sense, when I thought about it. There was absolutely no reason for us to be working in the same room otherwise."

What could Riley say to that?

He stared back, a sad smile on his face. "So I confronted her. She didn't deny any of it. Instead, she offered me a job. The kind of work we'd been doing, but more of it, and good money on top of that. They were impressed I'd scraped so much without getting caught. Basically, I'd passed their test."

"So when you say you turned down the job for ethical reasons…" Holy shit.

"Spying on armies and rebellions and organized groups trying to take down governments is different than peering into private lives because they might be selling government secrets—but probably aren't. We weren't working off a list of probable suspects. We watched *everyone* who had any connection to anything."

Riley couldn't hide her wince.

"Besides. Part of me still needs to prove…"

She waited for a moment. "What?" she asked when he didn't finish his sentence.

"Nothing." The single word was soft in the night. "Stupid shit."

A gust tore through the night, making her pull in tighter on herself. She saw the guilt and pain in his expression. Heard the hesitation in his words. He wasn't telling her everything, and whatever he held back devoured him. "Like what?" she asked.

"It doesn't matter." He drummed his fingers on his legs.

She felt the wall cropping up between them again. "Okay. It doesn't have to."

"I didn't mean to ruin your night with this." He stopped moving his fingers and clenched his jaw.

She expected some things to be tough for him to talk about, and this ate at him. "You didn't. I promise. I'm always here; that hasn't changed."

He forced out a breath through clenched teeth. "We should head home. You have to work in the morning."

"We can stay out here a little longer." She wanted to help him sort through this. As much as she'd tried to ignore it up to now, he wasn't the Zane who left six years ago. He was haunted by choices she couldn't fathom having to make, and she wanted to help him through it.

"And do what? Not talk? I'm sorry, Riley. I can't. Not tonight."

The shrug-off hurt more than she thought possible, gnawing inside and chipping away at her core. She wouldn't push him if he wasn't ready to talk, though. The only solution was for her to be available when that happened, and hope he understood she was listening without judgement.

"It's okay." It wasn't, but what else was she supposed to say? This wasn't about her. Zane needed to heal. "I understand."

chapter seven

Zane drummed his fingers against his leg, while he waited for Riley to answer the door. It was a good bet she was home. Her car was in the parking lot, and they were meeting Kenzie for dinner in a couple hours.

He told Riley he'd stop by early so they could just hang out for a little while. Still, no response to the doorbell or his knocking.

He hated to see her hurt, and it was worse when he knew he caused it—like the hurt reflected on her face after they left the bar two nights ago, when he couldn't bring himself to open up.

He was grateful she didn't push him, though. He'd made so many bad decisions while he was deployed, like every time he chose a challenge over what he knew was right.

Knock a third time, or call her? Oh, right. He grabbed his keyring. This would take some getting used to.

He pushed into the condo and locked the door behind himself. A movement out of the corner of his eye caught his attention, and he spun toward the kitchen. Riley sat at the table, sketchbook in front of her. With her earphones in, she was oblivious to the world.

He followed the curve of her body, from toes against the floor, up her bare leg, to where her thigh rested on the foot tucked beneath her. She wore a button-down shirt with only the middle two buttons done up, and possibly nothing else. Her half-dry hair hung around her face, as though she'd gotten out of the shower and forgotten to finish dressing.

She shifted her weight, and her shirt pulled open at the top, revealing a round, firm breast. His blood pressure kicked up a notch, and his cock throbbed. Her offer from the other night rushed back to him, taunting as it had so many times over the past few days. Fuck, she was tempting. Inspiration flushed her cheeks, and though she was half-exposed, she was still statuesque. Her focus made her that much sexier.

He really shouldn't be staring. He adjusted his jeans, doing his best to hide his reaction, and knelt next to her. She hadn't brought up the casual sex offer again. He'd have a hard time turning it down if she did. It was hard enough not bringing it up himself.

She had on more than just the shirt after all, though the plaid men's boxers peeking out from underneath did nothing to relieve the insistent throb below his waist. He ignored his arousal and rested a hand on her arm.

She almost jumped out of the chair, before she focused on him. Her hand flew to her chest, tugging her shirt farther open and offering an amazing view of her sun-darkened skin. "Holy shit. You scared the hell out of me."

He forced his gaze to her face, unable to hide a smile at her reaction. "Sorry."

"No, you're not." She tucked her legs under her again, covering more of her body with the shirt.

Not that the gesture did anything to stop the teasing images racing through his thoughts. "I kind of am."

"Sit next to me." She tugged him to his feet.

He dropped into a second padded chair, trying to be subtle about adjusting himself again. A tiny smile still danced on her lips. Was it because he wasn't succeeding at all in hiding his erection, or because she was still half-lost in her drawing? She gave him one last glance before turning back to her work. "How'd the interview go?"

His arousal limped away at the single question. "Not as well as I hoped." He hadn't even made it past the company's screening process, thanks to his lack of a degree or civilian experience. Those weren't the words used, but he heard it in the interviewer's voice over the phone and the way the conversation all but died when Zane mentioned his only experience with network security had been overseas for the military.

"I'm sorry," Riley said.

So was he. He also wanted to talk about anything else. He pulled her sketchpad toward him.

Wow. Awe raced through him. It was the character she said was based on him, with a wiry man kneeling in front of him. And both of them were naked. She hadn't told him she was drawing *yaoi*—male-on-male graphic novel pornography. "You drew another guy sucking me off?"

She let out a short laugh. "Since when are you a prude? Besides, it's not you. It's a drawing that happens to be built like you. I already told you that."

He should be offended or something, but the tease on her full lips, and that she'd drawn him naked in a compromising position—even if it wasn't one he was into—made his pulse race again. "I just don't get it. Why do some girls get off on two good looking guys groping each other?"

"I'm not getting off on it. And you're better? You've never fantasized about two women together?" She already knew the answer. She'd described for him over chat, at least half a dozen times, her making out with another girl.

The memory of the images she painted with words made his dick perk up. "That's different," he said.

"How?"

He provided the only answer he could think of—the truth. "Because one turns me on, and the other doesn't."

She planted both feet on the ground and scooted her chair closer to his. She nudged his knees apart, rested her elbows on her legs, and traced a line along his inner thigh. She didn't brush his erection, but she came close. "If it doesn't do anything for you, what are you right now?"

As hard as he had ever been. He couldn't keep his gaze off her chest and the fantastic view down the front of her shirt. He drew a finger along her collarbone, eliciting a sharp gasp. "That has more to do with you than your artwork."

"I thought you liked my drawing."

"Your skill is borderline erotic; it's true. The subject matter, not so much."

Mischief danced behind her eyes, and she increased the pressure against the inside of his leg. "You're telling me, if you've got a woman you're wild about, and she wants you and another guy at the same time…"

He grimaced—not at the idea, but because he was having a hard time focusing on anything but her touch and the gorgeous curves in front of him.

"Let me finish." Her voice was sultry and smooth. "You're telling me you wouldn't enjoy that at all? One of you between her legs, pounding away, and the other over her mouth, stroking himself, her tongue flicking out to caress his skin? That image doesn't do anything for you?"

"I'm not opposed to balls touching." It was hard to tell which visuals were doing what. All he knew was he'd need some sort of release before dinner. He was seconds from telling her exactly that, if it meant she'd help. "I'd rather be alone between your legs, eating you out."

A flush spread over her cheeks, but she didn't pull away. "I wasn't talking about me, and I call bullshit."

"Oh?" They'd had similar discussions before. Normally one of them backed down before things escalated, but his rushing blood and rock-hard erection wouldn't let him drop the subject.

She tucked her hair behind her ear, still stroking the inside of his thigh with her thumb. "Guys who insist they like giving oral better than receiving it only say so because they've never gotten a good blow job."

Fuck. What he'd give for a chance to prove her wrong. Or—hell—prove her right. "Tell me it's not the same for you. Maybe you've just never had a guy who knew what he was doing." He trailed off, half-expecting her to blow a fuse at the suggestion. When she raised her brows instead, he kept talking. "Besides, I never blame the girl. It's just harder to get me off orally."

"Bullshit. Again. I could so prove you wrong."

Every inch of him roared in response. The thought of her lips wrapped around his cock was almost enough to make him come on the spot. "Too bad we're not in a position to do that."

"You look like you're in the perfect position to me. You never gave me your answer the other day."

That saved him from bringing it up. "About?" He wanted to hear her say it again. Make sure they were on the same page.

"You know what about. Call it *friends with benefits*, if you want."

It didn't matter what they called it, as long as they kept the rules in mind. "Say I'm in." In her. On her. "We promise it's completely separate from our friendship?"

"Of course. We're both okay with it, and neither of us assumes it will or won't happen again. This is now, and every other moment is its own thing."

Yes, goddammit. Yes. He forced his tone to remain even. "All right."

"So the rules are simple. I bet I can get you off orally and you can't do the same. You name the prize."

"A screaming orgasm."

"You're on. Who goes first?"

He slid from his chair, done negotiating. He nudged her legs apart, scraping his fingers along the bare flesh of her inner thighs. Sharp cherry mingled with the scent of her sex, and his thoughts swam.

He kissed up the soft skin, the pain of anticipation straining against his jeans, when she moaned and arched her back. He glided his lips up one leg and down the other—from knee to knee—never moving past the edge of her shorts.

She whimpered and slid her butt forward in the seat. "You're a tease."

"And?" The need in her taunt made him smile.

"And nothing." She gasped when he kissed higher. "Just saying."

He lightly scraped his teeth over the cotton covering her mound, gliding his tongue along the fabric and over her covered slit. She whimpered again and shifted her hips closer.

He hooked his fingers in the elastic waist of her shorts and tugged. She lifted her ass off the chair long enough to let him slide the clothes to the floor, before she dropped back in her seat, legs spread.

He groaned at the sight in front of him. "Jesus. You're gorgeous."

She flushed and ducked her head.

He traced the outside of his finger along the edge of her pussy, his moan at how wet she already was mingling with hers. The promise of her taste taunted him, but he had a point to prove. The build-up was as important as the act itself. And he was going to make her scream.

Keeping his touch light, he parted her lower lips and followed a trail back down. Her skin glistened in the light.

He kissed up her leg until his mouth finally reached its destination. Her sweet taste hit his tongue, and his thoughts short-circuited. Better than the fantasy. Fuck. He wanted to bury his face down there and make her scream until she was hoarse.

Her breathing increased, and her hands rested on the top of his head. When he licked her clit, her gasp filled the room, and her hips bucked. His cock pressed against his jeans, begging to get in on the action, and he ignored it.

He wrapped his lips around her swollen sex, and she cried out. The new sound drilled into his head and jolted his dick. He flicked his tongue back and forth over the button, sometimes nipping lightly with his teeth.

She gyrated against him, her hands locked at the base of his neck. Part of him wanted to drop his pants and slide inside her, but even more, he wanted to hear her come like this. Wanted to taste her and feel her against his mouth when it happened.

He teased the edge of her entrance with his finger, still licking. Her whimper at the light contact melted into a loud moan when he pushed two fingers inside her. Jesus, she was slick. It was a good thing he still had his pants on, because once his cock came out, he wasn't going to last long.

He sucked harder on her clit, hooking up his fingers as he glided inside her.

She thrust forward again when he hit the right spot. "Fuck, Zane. God, yes."

Her breathing came in short gasps, and he nipped at her again, her sweet taste and the lack of blood to his head making the room swim. He pushed his fingers hard inside her. The thrusting of her hips grew to a frantic pace, and she held his head in place. Her ass rose off the chair, and her pussy clenched around his fingers as she came, squirming and driving against him, and groaning until he didn't know how she could still breathe.

Finally, she slumped back against the chair with a soft sigh.

He wanted to be smug, but even more, he wanted to bend her over the back of her seat and feel her tight pussy around his dick.

He rose to his knees, knotted his fingers in her hair, and crushed their mouths together. Kissing Riley was like nothing he'd ever experienced. Desire sparked in his veins at the taste of cherry lip-gloss mingled with her juices.

He could dive into this forever, dancing his tongue with hers. Nibbling her lips. Drowning in the hunger that flowed between them. How had they never even kissed before?

And how was he going to resist the urge to do it again? Fuck, he wanted her in a million different ways.

She pulled away, face flushed and eyes still heavy with want. "You were incredible."

"Told you." He smirked.

She nudged his shoulders, and he dropped back into his chair. She slid her fingers down the front of her shirt, undoing the few buttons holding it on, and dropped the clothing off her shoulders.

He couldn't pull his gaze from the gorgeous sight—the round tits, the curve of her hips, and the smooth spot between her legs.

She fell to her knees. "My turn."

The husky tone of her voice made his cock pulse harder. She made quick work of his belt, fingers brushing his bare waist as she undid the button on his jeans.

She pulled down his zipper, and he whimpered at the release in pressure. He groaned loudly at the skin-on-skin contact of her soft fingers working his shaft free from his boxer briefs.

She stroked him. "You're big. You never thought to mention that?"

"Show, don't tell. Right?"

She laughed and dropped her head, lips hovering less than an inch from his cock. He watched the deliberate, sensual movements, his pulse screaming. Her breath was hot against his skin.

"You don't mind"—she moved her lips up his length, still not making contact, and slid her free hand down her chest—"if I feel us both up. Do you? I wouldn't ask, but that thing you did with your tongue…" She looked up at him, her lip caught between her bottom teeth. "Just the thought of sucking you off… I'm still hot."

Every time he thought she couldn't unravel him further… "Please do."

She glided her tongue over the head of his cock. He growled when she dropped her hand between her legs at the same time she took him in her mouth, her groan vibrating through his skin. She moved slowly, keeping the tension high and him right at the edge, as she sucked.

Her sighs of pleasure increased, mingling with his. The sound of her voice blended with the look in her eyes, her mouth sliding up and down, and the sensation of her hand wrapped around him. All of them heightened every nerve ending in his body.

She pumped in rhythm with the bob of her head, hair spilling around her face and surrounding her in a curtain of blonde strands. He brushed her hair aside, needing to see her.

She increased her pace. Her muffled sighs and moans grew louder, and he recognized the sound of her drawing close to climax again. The noise drew him closer to a peak, taunting him, leaving his thoughts begging for release. She let her cries echo against his cock as she came, never slowing down.

He leaned back his head, so close to peaking but still not crossing that line. She caressed his sac, her fingers still slick from playing with herself, and he grunted in pleasure. She stroked the soft skin. Teasing. Tugging. Taunting. A rainbow wave spilled through his thoughts and filled his body. He felt a familiar clench in his gut and came fast and hard, all his thoughts vanishing in a rush when he hit the back of her throat with desperate thrusts.

She slowed as he did. As she pulled away, and licked him clean. He shuddered with each touch, his head still light from all the sensations.

She shifted her weight to sit on the floor, instead of kneeling, and folded her legs to the side. Pushing a strand of hair behind her ear, she rested her head against the inside of his thigh. Expectation and question shone in her gaze when it met his.

He let out a laugh, tinged with relief and disbelief. "Wow."

"So we call it a draw?"

He didn't care what they called it, as long as he got to keep the memory seared in his head. Still, he said, "A draw implies we get to try for a tie-breaker."

"I guess it does."

He trailed his fingers through her hair, watching the rise and fall of her chest. Memorizing how perfect this moment was. Did they really need to be somewhere else tonight?

She sighed. "We should probably leave soon."

"Yeah." That answered that. The bubble encasing them shattered.

She grabbed her shirt as she stood, pulling it on but letting it hang open. Her smile never faded. "I need another quick shower."

Fantasy ran rampant through his thoughts. "You want help?"

"Most definitely."

He closed the distance between them, tangled his fingers in her hair, and kissed her hard. His teeth crushed into his lips, and she groaned against his mouth. Yeah, he liked kissing her a lot. Good thing they hadn't taken another time off the table. Just the soft press of her lips was enough to make him half hard again.

He let go, not hiding his smirk when a tiny sigh escaped her lips. "Maybe next time," he said. "You don't want to hear it from Kenzie, for being late. But give me five minutes to clean up when you're done?"

"Sure."

He watched her walk away, hips swaying, the

shirt barely covering her ass. Reality rushed back in, and he sank into his seat with a grunt. *Please don't let this be a mistake*. The internal plea turned to a chanting voice, asking if he was being selfish again, doing what he wanted, regardless of who else was involved. True, the consequences for hurting Riley wouldn't be as severe as his last big mistake, but he'd never forgive himself if he were a cause of long-term pain for her.

chapter eight

Riley hit the next preset button on Zane's radio, and sighed at the bad memories the song summoned. She moved to the next station. Commercials. She tried one more time.

"Stop." There was no irritation in Zane's voice. He pressed the CD button, loosely grabbed her wrist, and set her hand back in her lap.

Her skin warmed when he didn't pull away immediately. He was incredible at her place. She'd never argue again that she didn't care for receiving oral. And those kisses… She could drown in those and never come up for air.

She'd found herself brushing her lips absentmindedly several times since.

But Zane hadn't said more than a couple words at a time to her since she got out of the shower. Which was exactly what she wanted to avoid. Maybe they'd pushed for too much too soon. They still hadn't found their footing after being apart so long.

A heavy techno beat filled the car, and she groaned. "Seriously?"

"You love this song."

She shrugged, though he was watching the road

and not her. "I did a decade ago."

"Sorry. I haven't had a lot of time to update my music collection." He skipped to the next track, and screaming electric guitar kicked in. "Better?"

She flopped back in her seat. They needed to talk about what happened between them. Or *she* did. For all she knew, his silence meant he'd already moved on, and she was the only one stuck in the moment. "Kenzie's going to know the minute she sees us," she said.

He glanced at her.

She tried to ignore the way his gaze briefly traced over her body, but she couldn't completely suppress her flush at the attention.

"Is that a bad thing?" He turned back to the road.

Riley loved her sister, but she didn't care for Kenzie's knowing glances. The insistence that one day Riley and Zane would end up together.

"I don't know. If it's not a big deal, we shouldn't have a problem telling her. Right?" Riley asked.

"That's really up to you. I'm not sure when your sex life became your sister's business, no matter how close you are."

"It's not. It's just that... Did you do *that* to placate me?" The moment the question spilled past her lips she regretted it.

He paused, as if measuring his response.

"Forget it. I never should have asked," she said.

"I meant it when I said you were incredible. In every possible way. And whichever *that* you mean? No. I didn't make you come, or enjoy every fucking minute of your lips wrapped around my cock, to placate you."

Now she'd offended him, on top of making things awkward. "Okay."

"I do a lot to see you smile, but I don't lie to you."

Relief crept in at the words. "I know. This is new territory to me. I'm still figuring out how I'm supposed to act."

Zane squeezed her fingers. It was amazing how such a simple gesture could still all the chatter in her head.

"Me too," he said. "But if nothing else is supposed to change, then we act like we always have. We don't have to tell Kenzie, because there's nothing for her to know."

Except something *had* changed. It wasn't only that the images dancing in her head were based on reality now. A new spark flowed between them each time he touched her. It wasn't a bad change, and the things he'd done with his tongue—she had no problem admitting she'd been wrong about being on the receiving end. They were still friends. But that whole *with benefits* thing added a new weight to the word. "I guess so."

"You know so, or it doesn't count."

"I know so."

He traced his thumb along the back of her hand. "So no big deal if it happens again?"

Oh, geez. A glow spread in her chest that she wasn't the only one hoping for a round two. Or more. "I wouldn't say that."

He gave her a sideways glance.

She wasn't writing off another chance at whatever they could get up to. "No big *bad* deal if it happens again. If next time is anything like this afternoon, it's certainly not insignificant."

"Fair enough." He let go of her hand to downshift and turn into the restaurant parking lot. A whisper of disappointment trickled through her at the missing contact.

They maneuvered through the parking lot looking for an empty spot. Riley recognized the familiar black Escalade in the front row as they approached, the G4M3G0D license plate making it hard to miss. She wasn't surprised Scott and Kenzie were already there. They were always at least ten minutes early.

"Game God? Really?" Zane snorted. "I wonder what kind of jackass drives that."

This wasn't quite how she'd wanted to continue a fantastic evening.

He glanced at her, as he pulled into a parking spot. "You're kidding."

"I told you. Kenzie landed herself a sexy rich guy."

"He's like… a programmer or something?" Zane fell into step beside her as they headed toward the restaurant.

She probably should have given Zane a little more information when she extended her sister's dinner invite. But the conversation took a random and she never got around to it. "Something like that. He's Chief Technology Officer, and co-founder of Rinslet Enterprises."

Zane's step faltered. "You mean *that* Scott

McAllister? How do you neglect to mention your sister is engaged to one of the biggest names in the industry?"

Sometimes Riley forgot Zane could be a fan boy. She tugged his hand to get him moving again. "Because I know him, and he's just another guy."

"Yeah, okay." He didn't sound convinced. He also didn't let go of her hand as they approached the entrance.

Kenzie looked at their intertwined fingers and then back at Riley, a knowing smile on her lips. Scott glanced at his watch.

Riley glared at her sister, hoping to convey this wasn't what it looked like.

Kenzie shook her head, still smiling, and turned to Zane. "Hey, stranger."

"Hey, yourself." He gave her a brief hug, both of them pulling away awkwardly.

Riley hid her laugh. Neither her sister nor Zane was ever physical, but it showed the most when they were together.

Introductions were made while Scott studied Zane, brow furrowed.

"They won't hold our table forever." Scott's tone was friendly but clipped.

Riley resisted the urge to ask what his problem was. He seemed to have lost the good humor she assumed was an integral part of him. She glanced at her sister. Kenzie's shocked expression probably mirrored her own.

"Right. Sure." Kenzie nodded toward the entrance. "We'll catch up when we're seated."

The steakhouse was packed with an eclectic

assortment of businessmen drinking and loosening their ties, families, and couples in jeans and T-shirts. Amber light diffused the white tablecloths, and the background music was lost in the chatter filling the room. Riley was grateful, as she usually was, that Kenzie and Scott didn't go for the higher-end places. She hated getting dressed up to go out to dinner, and she was glad someone had convinced her sister that wasn't necessary for a happy existence.

Scott was on a first-name basis with most of the staff, and they were seated quickly. Water and drinks were on their table within moments.

The conversation lulled, and Riley shot her sister a helpless look.

"Game God, huh?" Zane took a sip of his water, his tone casual.

"We can't all drive classic Beemers." Sarcasm laced Scott's reply.

Riley resisted the urge to roll her eyes. *Please don't let them do this.*

Zane clenched his jaw. It wasn't an obvious movement, but Riley had seen it enough times to know how irritated he was. His voice remained pleasant. "Not all of us have more money than God."

Scott's smirk grew. "I never really fell into the camp that deifies Bill Gates, but everyone has their own religion."

"And your religion is all about you?"

Damn it. Riley wasn't interested in the whole night being antagonistic. She let out a soft growl. "Put your dicks back in your pants, boys. You've already impressed everyone at the table."

Scott snorted.

"Riley Ann." Kenzie had the scandalized jaw drop down, Riley had to give her credit.

Riley glared back. "Mackenzie." Why couldn't Kenzie have a middle name too—something obnoxious, to be thrown back in her face? "Don't give me that shocked look. The two of you spend half your time throwing disgustingly lame innuendo at each other."

"Innuendo. Not crude locker-room insults."

Riley shook her head. "Your boyfriend's being an ass."

"Oops." Scott smiled when she glared at him.

Out of the corner of her eye, she saw Zane clench his hand into a fist. She knew her sister's fiancé was antagonistically honest, but for the first time since Riley met Scott, she was tempted to let Zane pound some politeness into him. She sought out Zane's knee under the table and squeezed, not sure if she was encouraging him or trying to calm him down.

Scott raised an eyebrow at the gesture, shook his head, and turned away from her glare. "You know I'm teasing, and maybe being a little overprotective of my baby sister."

Zane's frame stiffened, muscles going hard under her hand. His voice was calmer though. "No worries. It's cool."

Since Scott and Kenzie got engaged, he'd teased her about being the sister he never had, posturing about how he had to look out for her now. And Riley was used to Zane stepping to her defense. This was stupid though. Neither was a threat to her, nor competition to the other, so why were they acting like posturing morons with more testosterone than brains?

A memory from ages ago, before Zane enlisted, tickled the back of her thoughts. Something about a video game? The notion slipped away before she could grasp it.

Zane's posture relaxed, but she still felt tension thrumming through him. "Anyway... Riley says you're almost as important as you think you are."

"Not really. There are a couple of gamers who think so, and I let them believe it, to sell games, but I'm not."

And now everything was fine. Maybe they were both satisfied with the way they'd marked their territory? Riley didn't know.

"I've heard a lot of things about Rinslet, but the details are always vague. No one ever talks about more than how cutting edge you are. Rumor has it you've got an in-house rendering engine you designed," Zane said.

The thick air around the table seemed to be evaporating, so Riley wasn't going to push the issue. Besides, she loved listening to Zane talk shop. She always learned the most interesting things.

Scott nodded. "Yup. The rest is top secret. You know—I tell you, and I have to kill you. That kind of thing. Or hire you, to make sure no one else goes around leaking company secrets."

Zane flinched, the movement contrasting with his laugh. "You couldn't afford me."

Scott stared back, but it wasn't the challenging look he had earlier. There was more contemplation behind his gaze. "I'd offer you a company car and stock options, but something tells me you're not talking about money."

The offer caught Riley off-guard. Scott was generous, but he didn't bring people on unless he thought they could handle the job. Had Kenzie said something to him? There was no way her sister had talked Zane up enough to warrant *company car and stock options.*

"Nope," Zane said. He squeezed Riley's hand under the table, sending an unexpected warm flutter through her. Fortunately, no one's attention was on her, so no one would notice the pink flushing her cheeks.

Scott slid his business card across the table. "Call me if you change your mind."

The entire exchange made Riley's head spin, and she made a mental note to ask Kenzie about it later. She'd push the issue now, but the only way she could think of to phrase her concern came off sounding like *why did you just offer my friend a job? What's wrong with you?* Direct, and Scott probably wouldn't be offended, but there was no reason to talk Zane out of work options.

♥♥♥

Zane shoved the card in his back pocket. "You're not serious."

"Completely." Scott raised an eyebrow. "Unless you've already landed the perfect position. Kenzie says you haven't been stateside for long."

"I'll think about it." This was why Zane hadn't wanted to tell Riley he was having trouble finding work. Now she had her sister's fiancé trying to hook him up with some job born of pity.

"Are you done talking business at dinner?" A gentle warning ran through Kenzie's teasing tone.

"Yes, ma'am." Scott almost looked contrite.

Zane desperately wanted to be talking about anything but whether or not Riley went behind his back to drum up a job he hadn't earned. He spat out the first thing that popped into his head, grateful as the words passed his lips that it was a safe topic. "Has Riley told you what she's doing with her art?"

Riley dropped her hand from his knee and turned her narrowed gaze to her drink. The glass muffled her response. "No. I haven't really told anyone."

"Now I'm curious." Hesitation lined Kenzie's response.

Zane hated seeing Riley waste her talent. If his nudging wasn't enough to get her motivated, maybe Kenzie could help. "She's thinking of going pro."

The smile faded from Kenzie's eyes, though her lips stayed frozen. "That's a lot of work."

"You won't let me talk business at dinner." The irritation was back in Scott's voice.

Aggravation crept back into Zane. How had he forgotten this about Kenzie? If it wasn't mainstream, it wasn't the right way to do things. "Most things worth doing take a lot of work."

Scott picked at a piece of bread, pulling the crust off a bit at a time. "He's got a good point."

"Excuse me. I need some air." Riley pushed away from the table.

"You should probably not follow." Scott took hold of Kenzie's wrist when she stood.

Zane looked between the two of them, shook his head, and took off in the direction Riley had.

He found her pacing outside the front doors, her arms crossed, and a frown creasing her forehead. A gust of wind tore through the night, and she rubbed her arms. Her gaze was locked on the ground, and she didn't acknowledge him.

"Hey," he said to announce his presence.

She jumped and spun to face him, scowl still in place. "She's right. I'm spinning my wheels on this."

"She didn't say that."

"You know that's what she meant."

He swallowed the desire to argue but wasn't sure what to say instead.

"We should get back to the table." She ran the back of her hand over her eyes, wiping away invisible tears.

"We don't have to." He wanted to wrap her up in his arms and convince her Kenzie was wrong. "We'll bail."

The corner of her mouth pulled up. "No. It's okay. Just… I don't care what we talk about when we get in there. You and Scott can chest thump some more, for all I care. Just leave the drawing out of it?"

He didn't want to swear to something like that, but he felt backed into a corner.

"Promise me."

Make the concession to ease her mind, or push the issue and make the night more miserable? "All right."

A heavy silence descended over them, hovering when they rejoined Kenzie and Scott. The conversation was stilted the rest of the evening. Zane spent half his time worrying about Riley, and the other half trying to figure out what was safe to talk about. His frustration grew when they ordered dessert and Riley didn't try to steal even a bite of his cheesecake.

As they went their separate ways for the evening, Kenzie gave Riley an awkward hug. Zane kept his distance, hands shoved in his pockets. Scott kissed Riley on the cheek and whispered something in her ear. She shook her head and shrugged before stepping away.

"Hey." Scott caught Zane's eye and tugged him aside. "Thanks."

"For?"

Scott grinned, keeping his voice low. "Taking care of my baby sister."

Riley stepped up next to Zane, arm brushing his. "Good night."

Kenzie gave her one last sad look, and then let Scott lead her in the other direction.

Riley fell into step next to Zane. He held open the truck door for her, still at a loss about how to bring her smile back.

chapter nine

Riley managed to swallow most of her discomfort on the short drive back to her condo. She'd been embarrassed when Zane brought up her artwork. She shared the dream with him in confidence, thinking it would stay between them until she was ready to make things public. Then Kenzie had to go and confirm her worst fears. Zane was just being polite when he said she was talented, and the entire thing was a total waste of time.

She didn't want to spend the night wallowing. She needed a distraction. Zane pulled into the visitor parking, and she spat out the question before she could stop herself. "Do you have anywhere to be in the morning?"

"Not really."

"Stick around for a while. We'll game or something."

"I'm in." He shut off the truck and followed her inside.

Riley kicked the door shut and leaned back against it, not sure what to say. Telling herself not to think about the disappointment of the night proved to be the best way to think about that and only that.

Zane studied her face for a moment, a shadow tinting his eyes. He grabbed her fingers and tugged her toward the couch. "Scott calls you baby sister?"

She flopped next to him on the cushions. A brief flash of uncertainty pulsed through her, and she decided at the last minute to keep a few inches between them. "I'm younger than he is, and we'll be related by marriage soon. He thinks it's a funny nickname, because I'm the older twin."

"I guess that makes sense. Just make sure he understands I'm the one who gets to knock skulls and bust kneecaps if someone hurts you."

The protective words warmed something deep inside her, and at the same time made her gut clench. "I'm not exactly living a life of danger."

Silence stretched between them, the way it did far too often recently. He fidgeted, rubbed his hand over his head, and sighed several times. He might be talking about Scott, but that wasn't where his mind was.

"What are you thinking about?" she asked.

He shifted on the couch, turning to face her and tucking one foot under the other knee. "The day I packed up and left for MEPS."

She searched for some hint in his expression, but an impassive gaze stared back at her. She remembered when he shipped off for boot camp. How hard it had been to say *goodbye* at the airport. How something had been off. She'd assumed it was that his entire life was about to change.

"I couldn't sit still that morning. Watching the clock, waiting… And then it was almost time to go. I looked everywhere for Granddad and finally found him on the back porch."

Zane's mother passed away when he was eight. That had been the most horrible summer Riley remembered from their childhood. He withdrew completely, and it took months to get him to talk again. His grandfather had raised him after that.

She always thought the older man was odd, even overly strict. Like when Zane was nine and had complained he was too big for his bed. The next night his bed had vanished, and he spent almost a month sleeping on the floor.

When his granddad replaced the missing bed—with something very high-end, at least for a nine-year old—he said something like, *The difference between knowing a thing and understanding a thing is complacency.*

Regardless of his quirks though, the man was always kind to Riley, and Zane saw him as a father, so she gave him some leeway.

"And?" she asked.

"He didn't say anything for several minutes." Zane rested his arm on the back of the couch, staring at something past her she knew she wouldn't see if she turned around. "I've never forgotten what he said when he spoke."

She couldn't help but frown at his distant look, and didn't dare interrupt the half-memory.

"He told me my mother had always had an uncanny talent for bringing joy and comfort to those who needed it." He clenched and unclenched his fist. "That he'd known from the time I was five that I wouldn't be the same."

"That's not fair." A wave of fury rose in her.

He held up his hand. "He was right."

"No."

Zane gave a tiny smile. "He told me people like us—him and me—that it was our personal responsibility to see that people like Ma"—he trailed off and then finally gave her his full attention again—"and *you* always had that opportunity. That men like me were born evil, and that was our redemption."

"What does that mean?" Riley couldn't fathom a person saying something so cruel, especially to someone they'd raised as a son. "You're not evil. You're as far from it as possible."

"Are you sure? I've thought about that a lot since." His face was devoid of emotion. Which was a little eerie, considering the haunted look he'd worn so much lately. "You know how I spent my life before I enlisted. Just because I wasn't shoplifting or mugging people doesn't mean I wasn't a thief. I stole electronic versions of games. I hacked security systems, because I could, and took what most would call insider information, to see how it would play out on the stock market."

"But..." She struggled for an argument, but it was true. Those things had been wrong. She still didn't get *evil* from them, though.

"Enlisting gave me permission to do it legally."

"Except you walked away," she said. "You hit that point where you knew it was wrong, and you left."

"Walked away. Right. Granddad said the job offer was coming too. That people with my gray-area ethics were sought after. That someone would buy me, and they'd meet my price."

Riley didn't know what to do with the information. She did know there was too much pain and self-doubt associated with it, and she couldn't even begin to touch it. "Except they couldn't buy you. If he were right, you'd have taken the CIA job."

"Right. Exactly. I turned them down." His words sounded hollow. Lacked conviction.

Zane couldn't have done anything *too* bad. He was lost in a guilt she didn't understand but wanted to help erase.

She leaned her head on his arm. "If that's all that happened, it's not a big deal." *Is it all that happened?* The question stuck in the back of her throat. It was rude to ask, but a tiny voice said maybe she was terrified he'd give her an answer other than *yes*.

He didn't look convinced, and the haunted look of the memory lingered in his gaze. "But what if I'd done something else?"

"You don't have to keep that stuff to yourself. I'm always here to listen. I know you look up to your granddad, but he's wrong about this. You're not evil."

Whatever doubts nagged in the back of her mind, they didn't deserve her attention. Zane needed her. He'd do the same for her, not that she could imagine being that lost in her past or keeping it to herself if she was.

She stood, ignoring the question on his face, and pulled his foot out so it was straight on the couch. She turned her back to him and sat between his legs. Pulling his arm around her, she settled her back against his chest. Maybe he didn't need the comfort, but after a revelation like that, she didn't know how someone couldn't. She was relieved when he didn't pull away.

"Enough about my demons." His voice was low when he spoke again. "Tell me what you got up to while I was gone."

She felt selfish. He carried an invisible weight on his shoulders, and she was going on about things like art and whether or not she knew what love was. If he wanted to change the subject, though, she wouldn't push back. "That's an open-ended question."

"So pick something to start with, and we'll go from there. Like what made you decide to get more serious about the manga or work or anything. Except maybe Archer. I think I know enough about that."

She pulled his arms tighter around her. Maybe if she wrapped them both in normalcy, it would help. "Well, it did start in his comic shop…"

He stiffened.

"I promise, that's where the Archer part of things ends." She drifted into the explanation. In the back of her mind, Zane's story about his past still taunted her. Not only what he said, but the things he kept to himself. And as much as she tried to pretend it wasn't there, the nagging voice in her skull knew it gnawed at him, and wondered if he'd be able to handle whatever he hid before it devoured who he was.

chapter ten

Riley blew a loose strand of hair off her forehead and let the tension of the workday melt away. She loved handling accounts, helping customize benefits packages, and working with clients, but it still took a lot out of her.

She wove her way through the pack of coworkers leaving for the day, pausing for the occasional car before continuing toward her own. It was a gorgeous evening—sun, a few clouds, and the perfect temperature. Too bad she'd been stuck inside for most of it.

Her exhaustion melted away as she rounded the corner in the aboveground parking garage and her car came into view. She couldn't hide her smile at the unexpected sight of Zane leaning against the hood, legs crossed at the ankles and hands shoved in his pockets. The casual posture elongated his thin frame but drew the eye to the definition under his shirt.

Too bad they were somewhere public. Memories of their bet the other night mingled with fantasy and teased her with possibilities. He met her halfway and wrapped an arm around her waist to steer her in a different direction. This was much better than the Zane who was lost in a world she couldn't reach.

She leaned into the warmth, unable to hold back her amusement. "Do we have plans?"

"We most certainly do." He stopped next to his truck and held the passenger door open for her.

A brief image raced through her thoughts of him pressing her against the door, pulling her hair, and kissing her hard. It sent a tingle to her belly. She tried to push the feeling aside but didn't manage completely. She slid into the seat.

"Do I get to go home and change first?" she asked as soon as he was seated.

"Nope. I can't give you a chance to decide not to go."

"I can't decide not to go if I don't know what we're doing."

He nodded to something behind the seats, and then backed the truck out and navigated with the rest of the after-work traffic. "Drawing."

She arched her brows when she saw what he was talking about. "Why do you have my sketchpad?"

"You mentioned the other day that you were stuck. That you were trying to draw poses you couldn't see clearly in your head. I'm going to help you picture them. Where to?"

She was doing just fine right now, visualizing him in a number of poses. Towering over her. Sliding up behind her. Pinning her arms back… That wasn't what he was talking about. "Copperton." She wanted to be irritated he'd sprung this on her, but at the same time, it warmed her that he remembered, and she'd already put off getting more reference photos for too long. "I don't need my sketchbook for that."

He glanced at her longer that time, something unreadable in his expression. "Really?"

"You know I always draw from photos." Fortunately she could take those with her phone. "You can still model for me."

"See?" He turned down a highway, taking them away from the rush hour traffic and heading toward the destination she'd given him. "So it's not a bad idea."

"Not even close."

He tapped out a tuneless rhythm against the gearshift. "Once you have these, how long until you finish your portfolio to a point where you're comfortable sharing?"

Her gut clenched at the question, chasing away some of her fantasies of the kinds of poses she wished she could put him in. It wasn't the asking that bothered her; it was the actual doing. Submitting meant showing new people her work. What if she got her stuff out there and realized she was average at best? "I don't know."

"You have *some* idea."

She trailed her thumb over her fingernails one at a time, and then repeated the gesture. "I have an entire graphic novel finished, except for some clean up. The reference shots are for Book Two."

He nodded toward her sketches behind the bench seats. "It's all in there?"

She tried to force away the nervousness the idea filled her with. "It is."

"Do it." There was a stern edge to his teasing.

She flushed, not sure which to focus on—the pleased feeling of the encouragement, or the terror of showing a stranger her artwork. "Soon."

The conversation shifted and tripped from topic to topic as they navigated the back roads. When they reached Copperton, she gave him a series of twists and turns through the small town. She'd always loved it up here. There were trees everywhere, and the surrounding mountains drowned out the heavy noise of a growing city. Most of the roads were two-lane, and she didn't know if there was a stoplight in the entire place.

Several years ago, she found a spot away from it all. A clearing with packed dirt, surrounded by trees, and devoid of anything but nature. She was surprised but pleased it had remained untouched after all that time. She directed him to park as close as he could without leaving the packed dirt path that led past it.

He stood at the back of his truck, hands shoved in his pockets. "Where do you want me, boss?"

Wherever you want to have me. She pushed the thought aside with a flush and pulled down the tailgate. "Sit."

He flopped into the back of the truck, kicking his legs back and forth, resting his elbows on his upper thighs. "You have to be more specific."

In the past, she'd always just asked him to send her photos. Then again, he hadn't been right there to pose as she needed, and she did have a couple of specific angles she really wanted to get. "Pull your knee up."

He pulled his knees to his chest, and rocked

back and forth.

"Not like that."

"Show me."

She closed the distance between them and tugged one leg down, then pushed the other back up so his foot sat on the truck bed. He hissed when she ran her hand along his thigh. She was tempted to move higher rather than lower, but that wouldn't accomplish what they were there for. Next, she trailed her fingers along his arm and draped it over the knee.

She forced herself to step back, rather than feel him up. She pulled her phone out and snapped photos from as many different angles as she could. Moving around him, studying the way the sun caught his form and cast shadow and light in all the right places, was enough to draw her into the moment.

That was the easy shot, though. The reason she liked the isolated clearing was the ground was almost always covered with leaves or pine needles, and though there were houses and streets just a few blocks away, they weren't visible through the trees.

If she could capture the silence of the area on camera, she'd do that as well. There was the occasional roar of a distant engine, but for the most part, only the squawk of birds pierced the air.

"Over here next." She spoke softly, not wanting to disrupt the ambiance. When Zane was within reach, she tugged him to stand next to her. His warm palm against hers was a pleasant contrast to the creeping chill as the sun drifted behind the mountains.

"Crouch down." She nodded at a pile of pine

needles nearby.

"Like this?" He crossed the short distance to the new spot and sat on his heels, arms on his knees.

"Not quite, but good start." She had an image in her head, and she knew he was capable of pulling it off. But it wouldn't be easy to describe. She knelt in front of him. "Don't fall."

"Why would I—whoa."

She trailed a hand down his left leg, pushing until it was almost straight behind him. His muscle was taut under her grip, and when she pulled away, she did so with reluctance.

She shifted to crouch behind him and nestled her chin on his shoulder. His familiar scent taunted her as she glided her hand along his arm. Her chest molded against his back as she finished posing him.

"I can think of someplace else for that other hand, if you want." His voice was low and deep.

Her laugh faded into a sigh when he grabbed her free wrist and tugged it over his shoulder.

He kissed along the inside of her wrist, his mouth soft and undemanding. His breath tickled her senses. "If I'd known you were going to twist me into so many angles, I might have negotiated to do the same in return before I agreed to this."

"This was your idea." It took all her willpower to extract herself and stand. It wasn't the kind of pose she wanted him to have to hold for long. "But you should have negotiated. I would have agreed."

"Oh." His disappointed groan mingled with a wounded laugh. "Now you tell me."

She winked before she took more pictures. "Something to keep in mind next time." This was too easy with him, and she didn't mind a bit.

The evening light vanished, and they had to pull a lantern from the back of his truck to keep working. That was fine with Riley. She used the new lighting to grab shadow effects that would make for fantastic references.

A breeze swept over her, and she shivered. She glanced at her phone. "Holy shit. It's after nine."

Zane climbed to his feet and stretched his arms above his head, elongating every muscle in his torso. "I think I owe you dinner."

She strolled toward the truck, saying over her shoulder, "You did me the favor. Doesn't that make it my treat?"

"Not sure I follow your logic."

"All right. Whatever."

He grabbed her wrists and pulled her toward him. "You're sure you got everything you need?" His breath brushed the outside of her ear.

"Everything art-related," she said. His warmth flooded her, his scent summoning the images that had taunted her off and on since he'd picked her up.

He pressed his entire frame against hers, nudging her back a step but not letting go. "Promise me you'll do something with it."

"Of course."

"Soon. Like actual *soon*. Not like a generic thing you keep putting off one more day."

"I promise." She probably would have promised him anything just then, with the power in his grip and his genuine interest in her work. The heat between them called to a growing need between her legs.

"Good girl." He smirked and spun, twirling them both so her back was to the side of the truck.

She squealed in surprise. Her laughter caught in her throat when she realized how serious his expression was.

He dipped his head and ran his lips up her neck, barely brushing the skin. "Since you think you owe me something, can I call in a favor besides dinner, for being a good sport?"

She sighed and tilted her head back, sinking into the feather-light kisses. "It was your idea."

"So you're not grateful?" His hurt tone was disrupted by the tease running underneath.

"I'm incredibly grateful." She shifted her weight from one foot to the other, rubbing against him. "Name your price."

He let go of her wrists without warning, moving to tangle one hand in her hair. He tugged her head back and grazed his teeth over the sensitive skin of her throat.

She whimpered at the hunger and aggression, digging her nails into his back to keep her balance. He pulled her hair harder, pressing his mouth to hers and muffling her moan. He plunged his tongue into her mouth and danced it around hers.

She caught his bottom lip between her teeth when he pulled away. Pressing against him, she rubbed her hip against his hard arousal. Going down on him the other night had been fun, but she wanted to know what it felt like to have him inside her.

He dropped his hands to her hips, guided her to the back of the truck, and lifted her up to sit on the tailgate.

"My price is steep." He sucked and bit hard along the soft flesh of her neck. He pushed a knee between hers, forcing her legs apart and her skirt higher up her thighs.

"It's worth it." Her response was breathy.

He slid his fingers down the front of her shirt, undoing buttons as he went, and drew a wet trail with his mouth on the now exposed skin. She reached for the waistband of his jeans, and he grabbed her wrists again and pinned her hands to the bed of the truck.

His growl echoed in her head, and his mouth grazed her ear. "Not yet."

"Yes, sir." Her pulse raced in response. Her sex grew slick.

He pressed his lips against her chest, his chuckle rumbling through her skin. "I like the way that sounds."

So did she.

He let go of one wrist to glide his rough palm up her stomach until his thumb brushed the bottom edge of her bra. She whimpered and arched her back to get closer. They might be out of the main flow of traffic, but they were still in public. The realization notched her heartrate higher.

He pushed up her bra, elastic scraping her skin. Cold air rushed in around the exposed region. Her whimpers blended into a gasp when he wrapped his lips around her hard nipple. Desire thrummed through her at the hunger in his movements. Each new suck, nibble, and flick of his tongue drove her senses wild.

He moved his mouth to her other breast, licking and biting the tender flesh. She scooted her butt forward on the tailgate, her skirt sliding up to her hips when she wrapped her legs around the back of his knees and drew him closer.

His laugh vanished into a groan when she pressed against him through his jeans. He kissed her hard, crushing his mouth against hers.

Lost in the onslaught of sensations, she was only vaguely aware of him pulling a condom from his wallet, his mouth never leaving hers. Part of her wondered why he'd been prepared with protection, the rest of her didn't care.

His hand brushed her mound through her panties when he reached between them to undo his jeans. He held her in place while he rolled on the rubber, and swallowed her moans when he pushed her underwear out of the way with the head of his cock and nudged her slick opening.

"I love how wet you get." He bit into her shoulder, drawing another gasp, and then plunged inside her.

She tightened her legs around him at the sudden penetration, and ran her nails sharply up his back. He dropped his hands to her waist and held her as he rocked against, her slowly at first, but steadily increasing his pace.

Each time he moved inside her, he hit her G-spot. As the rhythm increased, her climax built. Her breath came out in short gasps as she drew closer. He pumped harder against her, pushing her over the edge. Her orgasm washed over her, and she tightened her grip, milking his cock.

His breaths became grunts, and she recognized the sound of him getting close. She kept pace with his thrusts as he peaked and then slowed.

He buried his forehead against the still-tender skin on her neck, and she gasped at the whisper of pleasure and pain.

"I think I left a mark." His chuckle was tired, his voice muffled.

She leaned more of her weight on her hands, slowly unwinding from him. "I hope so."

He tangled his fingers in her hair again and pulled hard to press his lips to hers. When he let go, he didn't move away. "Feel free to use me any time."

"For modeling," she said.

A heavy flush tinged his tanned cheeks from exertion and the chill of the creeping night. "Sure. Whatever you want to call it."

She wanted to stay wrapped up in him forever. The moment the thought passed through her mind, she regretted it. That wasn't what this was about. There was no way she was falling for Zane. She'd promised herself. She'd promised him. This feeling was misplaced. She wasn't making that mistake again, especially since another good friendship was at stake. It wasn't love; it was incredible sex with a guy who understood what she wanted.

Her phone buzzed, the vibration rolling through the truck bed and startling them both. She laughed, as much at her own response as to push away the downward spiral of her thoughts. "Completely forgot about the real world for a minute."

He tugged her skirt down. "Do you think it's important?"

She grabbed her phone from her purse. A hint of her euphoria evaporated when she read the text.

"Archer."

Zane sighed and turned away, to strip off his protection and make himself decent. "And?"

She looked between the message and him. The space between them was cavernous, and she wanted Zane back by her side. Wanted to bury her face in his chest again. She shook aside the longing. This was sport sex, and they were in the middle of nowhere. It wasn't like they were going to cuddle after. "He wants to know if you asked me and what I think. Asked me what?"

He clenched his jaw.

She didn't like the reaction, but she wasn't letting herself pretend they were a couple. Another friend asked for her attention. "I can find out from him."

"He's got midnight premier tickets tonight for the new superhero movie. When I was on my way out, he asked if we wanted to go."

She'd been to all of those movies with Archer. She'd completely forgotten about this one. "Do you?"

"You've seen all of them, and I know you weren't just being polite."

"We're all going, right?" She texted a reply to Archer as she spoke. They were acting normal. That meant she'd go.

Zane pursed his lips, and then a smile forced its way out. "Of course."

chapter eleven

Hot to *friend* in two-point-three seconds. Riley had filled the empty space with chatter since they left the clearing forty-five minutes ago. Every time Zane glanced at her, she was staring out the window. He gripped the steering wheel and kept his attention on the parking lot, scanning for a spot in the sea of cars. It was probably a good thing they decided there wasn't enough time to stop for dinner. He was tempted to skip the movie and rediscover the moment they had up the clearing, but he knew Riley was looking forward to the film.

She was out of the car the moment he parked, a skip in her step as they made their way to the theater. Except he saw the stutter to her gait, as if she was trying too hard.

He wanted to wrap his arms around her and hold her close and tell her whatever it took to calm her down. Except that wasn't his role or his right. Spending time with her when she was diving straight into the world around her and laughing and living was respite for Zane. It chased away the dark shadows always lurking at the front of his mind, and made him think life went on.

The way her mood shifted to awkward and unsure after they had sex, or when he pushed her too hard to pursue her dreams, made the demons and doubts race back. Not only because his mind was free to trip over the past again. Her change in behavior haunted him with a single question—*Am I being selfish again?* Nudging her toward discomfort just to distract himself?

He shook the thoughts aside, though not as effectively as he had the last few times, and focused on Riley again.

Her forced skip slowed when Archer came into view. She crossed the last few feet to him, already talking, a lilt to her voice. "I can't believe you got tickets. You. Rule. Me."

Relief trickled through Zane when she didn't throw her arms around Archer's neck, but he still wished she wasn't so on edge.

Archer shoved his hands in his pockets, looking between the two of them sheepishly. "It didn't make sense to ignore this one. I'd have been wounded if you couldn't make it." He fixed his gaze on Zane for a minute, eyes hardening, before turning back to Riley. "Tori's holding our place in line. Did you already eat?"

"I'm good. I don't think I could stomach popcorn this late at night." Riley spun so she faced them both, and reached for them but dropped her hands at the last minute. "Let's go watch someone sexy and arrogant with as much brains as balls save the world." She walked backward, talking and glancing over her shoulder occasionally to keep from running into something.

"Did I miss something between you two?" Archer stepped closer to Zane, voice low.

Great. Other people saw her tension too. "Nope." He kept his expression neutral and his response quiet.

Riley met Zane's gaze one last time before turning away, uncertainty and something else hiding in her blue eyes. She made a straight line for a spot in the pockets of people stacked against one of the theater walls. Tori straightened as they approached. Her long hair was piled on her head and her glasses pushed up her nose, and she looked as friendly as when Zane first met her two weeks ago, when she delivered Archer a themed dress she made for one of his customers.

Riley bounced up next to her. "I'm so glad I won't be drooling over the sexy guys alone."

Tori laughed. "I was worried you wouldn't make it."

"Wouldn't have missed it."

"For real," Archer said to Zane. "What did you do? Sleep with her or something?"

Zane bit back his growl. "I didn't do anything."

Riley's shoulders rose and fell when she sighed, and she turned back to face them.

"First of all"—she turned an icy stare on Archer—"none of your god damned business. Second, I'm standing right here. I can hear you."

Archer at least had the grace to look sheepish. Tori refused to look at anyone. Zane wasn't surprised there. She spent a lot of time with Archer, though Zane knew they weren't dating, but she was the opposite of confrontational.

"I invited Mikki," Archer said. "But she couldn't make it."

Talk about awkward ways to change the subject. "Why?" Zane hadn't realized she was anything more to Archer than a customer.

Riley's frown deepened. Was that even possible? "She's the cutie with the short hair and barbell?"

"The one who worships Zane. Exactly." Tori nodded.

"She… what?" Riley's expression shifted to hurt and then a blank mask in a blink.

And reality crashed in around Zane. Jesus, he was dense. Archer was trying to hook him up. With someone who wasn't Riley.

How did this all get so fucked up so fast? "It's probably for the best. She seems nice enough, but no one wants to be the fifth wheel."

Archer scowled.

Riley relaxed more than she had since they arrived, and the corner of her mouth tugged up.

He wanted to turn that into a full-blown smile. And do so much more. But that wasn't his right. He really needed to wrap his brain around his own feelings.

♥ ♥ ♥

"Be right back." Tori's whisper barely carried over the explosions on screen. They were in the center of the aisle, which meant Riley didn't have to move, but everyone else down the aisle did.

Riley gave her a half nod. With Tori on one side and Archer on the other, she felt too far from Zane.

Which was good—or was it bad—since she still regretted ending the earlier part of their night so abruptly. She was reading too much into things. The entire point of fooling around with Zane was to keep her from thinking she'd fallen for yet another guy.

She couldn't believe how much it hurt though, when Archer implied Zane might hook up with Mikki. Riley felt like her heart had been squeezed into a tiny ball.

But to realize Zane hadn't even seen it coming. To hear him brush the entire idea off… She'd been so relieved.

When someone dropped into the seat next to her, she glanced to see if it was Tori, or someone she should evict. When she saw Zane, her heart fluttered, and she turned her attention back to the screen. Despite her half-assed attempt to ignore him, the heat of his arm a few inches from hers and the familiar scent of his cologne made it difficult.

He set a box of Red Vines on her knee. His warm breath brushed her ear. "You should eat."

"Thanks." She kept her gaze forward, hating her body for reacting to the contact.

Out of the corner of her eye, she saw him intertwine his fingers in his lap and slump lower in the seat. She tapped her toes inside her shoes. She wouldn't make a big deal out of his gesture, even though he had brought her favorite candy, and it was reminding her she'd skipped dinner.

She couldn't help it. She tilted her head toward him and kept her voice low so she wouldn't disrupt anyone else. "How did you get Tori to switch seats with you?"

He kept his mouth near her ear, the heat filling her with another pleasant rush she didn't want to acknowledge. "Intercepted her in the hallway."

Warmth spread through her at the gesture that summoned memories of the afternoon in the mountains. She already had trouble focusing on the on-screen love interest, who would almost definitely be gone by the next film in the franchise. "We're not a couple. We don't have to sit together." She loved that he did these things for her. The tiny acts without thought. But she didn't want him to feel obligated. Didn't like the voice asking if it was because they were screwing now, even though she knew it was something he'd always done.

"I know." The two words fell softly against her cheek. "But we would have before."

She tried to hide her smirk at the sound logic, and failed. "Touché."

He bumped his shoulder against hers. "Can I have some of your candy?"

She sank into her seat, arm next to his on the rest. "I guess. Just this once."

As the movie tore on, her mood continued to lighten. The four of them cheered with the rest of the crowd and booed and dragged their feet, waiting for that one tiny glimpse of the next film, as the credits rolled.

They stumbled into the night, and Riley paused outside, blinking while her eyes adjusted to the bright streetlights lining the parking lot.

"So"—Tori's exclamation was loud in the still night—"Mr. Rich-but-Arrogant in the costume. Absolutely hot."

"I could wear a costume." Archer's feigned hurt was exaggerated.

"You would be just as irritating as he was," Riley pointed out. "Ms. Sexy-Spy-Lady? I would love to be able to fight like that." She kicked into the air and promptly stumbled over a crack.

Tori caught her and pushed her upright again. "Get Zane to teach you. He's got the mad moves, right?"

An unexpected flush coursed through Riley, along with images of some of the moves Zane had shown her so far. She ducked her head, hoping her thoughts didn't show on her face. "I'm not nearly that coordinated."

"But"—Zane interjected—"you'd look a million times better in the black leather than she did."

"He's right." Tori turned to walk backward, studying Riley. "I could absolutely make you something like that. I bet Archer would pay you just to stand around the store in it. Can you imagine the draw?"

"I can imagine cleaning the drool off the glass counters." Archer didn't sound bothered. "I'd still let you do it."

The attention drew Riley's embarrassed flush out further. She was having too much fun to spoil the moment, but she wanted a subject that wasn't her. "I can't believe it's after three. I am so tired and so wired. I won't get anything done at work tomorrow. Or is that today?"

"So call in sick," Zane said. "I'll forge you a doctor's note."

Archer held up his hands. "I don't want to hear

anything about the two of you playing doctor."

Riley feigned an exhausted stumble, a bit for fun, and a bit to indicate the tiredness was sinking in. Warmth flooded her veins when Zane caught her. She pushed upright again. "Seriously. I need coffee. We should go to Denny's. If I have to work in the morning anyway, why sleep?"

"I can do Denny's." Archer pulled his keys from his pocket. "I'm with Zane, though. Call in sick. Stop by the shop and pick up the stack of manga I've been holding for you. Unless you've got something better to read."

Riley was about to agree, when Zane cut in. "I'm guessing reading someone else's work isn't the same, when you've got your own to focus on."

The warm fuzzies flitting through Riley beat a rapid escape but didn't take her embarrassment with them. *Please don't let him do this*. Her gut sank. "Denny's?"

"Wait. Really?" Archer studied her, curiosity and doubt in his hazel eyes. "Are you doing more than just dabbling now?"

"She's going pro." Zane smirked.

She was going to kill him. Or something. Why was he doing this to her? The private support was one thing, but getting friends and family to gang up on her, bombarding her with so many expectations, when she didn't even know if she had what it took to make it, was too much.

"For real?" Archer raised an eyebrow. "Are you sure?"

She furrowed her brow. How was she supposed to respond to that? "I haven't decided yet. It gets difficult to pick a direction, when someone"—she glared at Zane—"keeps telling everyone before I've made up my mind."

Zane frowned and turned away.

"You know he's biased." Archer didn't back down. "It's really hard to make it in that market. You can't be *good*. You have to be the *best*."

Zane's eyes narrowed. "She is the best."

"She's good." Archer shrugged. "I'm just saying."

"Well, don't," Zane said.

Riley's good mood evaporated, the truth of Archer's words sinking in. Maybe suggesting they all go for coffee was a bad idea. Exhaustion overtook her thoughts, pushed on a wave of Archer's doubt. He might be a lot of things she didn't like, but he also never sugarcoated the truth, the way Zane did. Archer had a point. She'd have to be the best, and she wasn't.

chapter twelve

Riley didn't want to go through the front door. She didn't want to do this in front of Archer and every other customer in the shop, but Zane was in there, behind the counter, not looking quite genuine as he laughed with his friends. She pushed inside, and Archer grinned.

"Hey. Are you here for the manga after all?" he asked.

She was there for her drawings, but she knew that wasn't what he meant. She looked at Zane, hoping her expression conveyed how desperately she didn't want to discuss details. "Technically."

Zane straightened up. "Hey."

"I need back that thing you borrowed yesterday." It took a force of will to keep the tension from her voice. She didn't care that Zane still had her sketchpad; she didn't want to talk about it with an audience. Her ego was bruised enough without another dig from Archer. But asking if she and Zane could talk privately would expose as much of her.

"So this is what it's like to be on the outside of her vague questions." Archer looked back and forth between them, his tone too light given the tension in the room.

Zane rolled his eyes and turned to Riley, expression softening. "It's in my apartment."

"Sounds perfect." She ignored the way Archer clenched his jaw, and followed Zane upstairs. When he held his apartment door open for her, she brushed past without a word, pacing the short distance between the living room and kitchen areas before turning on her toe and heading in the other direction.

He leaned back against the door, hands in his pockets. "Tell me what's wrong."

"Nothing. Just… Nothing. I need my sketchpad back."

He kicked away from the door and crossed the room to stand next to the kitchen table, directly in her pacing path. "It's obviously not nothing."

"You think?" She came up short, a few feet back. "You really can't figure it out?" An irritation she hadn't realized was there surged forward.

He shrugged.

"You can't just go around telling everyone what I'm trying to do with my art."

"I won't, if you ask me not to, but can I at least know why?"

She clenched her teeth. How could he not get it? "Because of conversations like this. Because even though it's awesome that you support my decision, you don't understand what it takes. Kenzie and Archer—they don't get it. Every time they voice their opinion, it's another layer of doubt, taunting me and telling me I'm making a mistake. It's more pressure, and doesn't help that I'm terrified of showing my work to a lot of people."

The confession was out, and though it left a gnawing in her gut, it also felt good.

The corners of his mouth drooped. "I didn't realize."

She sighed. "I adore you—you know it—and I'm flattered you think I'm talented. I'm not sure you're right, but I like hearing it."

He closed the distance between them. "You should have told me sooner."

"I'm telling you now."

His smile grew hopeful. "I promise I'll try to keep it all in mind. Are we're good again?" Zane asked.

She smiled. "Yeah, we're good again."

"Which means make-up sex." The way he raked his gaze over her, lingering on each curve, contradicted his teasing tone.

She couldn't help her relieved laugh or the flush of heat the idea brought with it. "Technically, I don't think we get make-up sex without a breakup, and we can't have one of those."

"Okay." He traced a finger down the side of her face. "Then best-friend sex."

"Is that a thing?"

He brushed his lips along the outside of her ear. "Isn't it? Besides"—his voice dropped an octave— "I can't stop thinking about how tight and wet you were last night. How you let me take control."

The confidence in his words made her skin tingle and her pulse race. "It was pretty amazing."

"Amazing." He trailed his fingers up her spine. "I like that. Would you let me do it again?"

Warmth spread deep in her belly. "Maybe."

"Uh-uh." He broke contact with her but didn't pull away. "*Yes*-or-*no* question. I know what I want, but I'm not doing it unless you're sure."

She swallowed, body humming in anticipation. "I'm positive."

Her comment was cut short when he nipped her bottom lip with his teeth. He twisted his fingers in her hair and pulled her back to him, crushing his mouth against hers. The smell of sweat mingled with the scents of musk and deodorant. An insistent need grew between her legs.

She covered his other hand and pushed it farther up her thigh, hooking her knee on his hip. Something whispered in the back of her mind that they couldn't keep toeing this line. She ignored it. This was exactly what she wanted. She needed to be closer to him.

He slid his hand along her ass and up over the curve of her hip, a chuckle rumbling in his chest. He moved his mouth back to her neck, his breath tickling her skin. "During the entire movie, I couldn't stop daydreaming about how it felt to be buried inside you."

The confession in his words made her thoughts melt and her skin ache for more. She fumbled for a good comeback, but her attempts failed when he grazed the soft spot between her neck and shoulders and sucked on the sensitive flesh.

He found the seam of her jeans that ran between her legs. She whimpered when he applied pressure with his fingers, rubbing her already wet slit through denim. She dug her nails into his back, squeaked, and shifted her weight until her aching button settled under his touch. He massaged harder, and she ground against his hand, feeling her climax build.

Her breathing came in short gasps, so many points of contact making her light-headed. Disappointment washed over her when he pulled away.

He kissed her pout and then moved to stand behind her, leaving her between him and the table. He brushed the outside of her ear with his lips and rested his hands on her stomach. "You trust me, right?"

She swallowed, mouth dry from anticipation, not doubt. She made sure her answer was clear, without any waver. "Yes."

His chest was hot against her back. "And you're okay with wherever this goes?"

"More than okay." Her heart hammered as a million images of what he meant taunted her simultaneously.

He tugged her shirt over her head and tossed it aside. "No bra. Makes this easier."

He moved his hands to her breasts and kneaded the soft flesh. She arched her back against him when he finally reached her nipples. He pinched both at the same time and fire spread through every inch of her. He bit the soft skin between her neck and shoulder, sucking in time to her moans. His hard arousal dug into her ass. She wanted more, but she also wanted to stretch the moment out and enjoy the prolonged teasing.

He dropped his hands to her waist, not fumbling at all as he undid her jeans. He hooked his thumbs over the waistband and tugged everything to the floor, leaving her exposed from head to foot, and binding her ankles.

Cool air rushed in around her, and her pulse pounded under her skin. She'd never had a guy take control like this before. She and Zane had talked about it several times. Now that it was actually happening, it made her head fuzzy, and she wanted more.

He cupped her ass before sliding his hand between her legs. "Fuck. You're so wet." His growl vibrated through her back.

"I think you had a lot to do with that." She closed her eyes, focusing on as many sensations as she could.

He massaged her slit, not dipping inside or reaching high enough to brush her clit. He placed his free palm against her spine and pushed her forward.

She did as prompted, bending at the waist and leaning over the table. The hard oak pressed into her chest and aching nipples. He held her in place. Her desire swelled when he dropped his hand from between her legs, and the faint but familiar sound of a zipper greeted her. A few seconds later, she heard the crinkle of cellophane.

He ran his hands from her shoulders down her arms, and pulled her wrists together. He grabbed both hands in one of his and pinned them in the small of her back. He spread her lower lips with his fingers, teasing her entrance.

She couldn't hold out much longer. "Please."

"Please what?"

"Fuck me."

He chuckled. There was no warning before he pushed inside, and her moan echoed off the table at the exquisite pain of being stretched out so much, so fast. He didn't let up, grunting as he pounded against her. The friction of having her legs together, combined with the spot he hit in her pushed her toward climax hard and fast. Her breathing came in short gasps, and she couldn't hold back the cries as she came.

She clenched around his cock, his erection buried deep inside her. She gasped when he found her clit at the height of her orgasm, and he rubbed the throbbing button. Part of her wanted to pull away, because it was almost too much, but the pleasure continued to assault her in waves. He slammed inside her, and her nipples scuffed against the wood grain with each new thrust. Another orgasm taunted her, bringing her right to the edge, but not further.

His breathing grew shallower, his thrusts more abbreviated and frantic. "I want you to come for me again." It was a command, not a request. Instead of teasing, he pressed his fingers roughly against her clit.

The sensation tore a climax from her, and she came hard, tightening around him. He pulled his fingers away from the now too-sensitive region between her legs. His grunts were fast and heavy, ending with the sound she knew so well and loved hearing on the phone. Hearing him get off was even better in person. The pounding slowed and then came to a stop.

He let go of her wrists and moved his hands to her hips as he and she struggled to catch their breath. She pushed up to her elbows, wincing as her legs wobbled and threatened to give out. He collapsed into a nearby chair, and was tender, helping her find her balance, and then tugging her to sit on his lap.

She rested her head on his shoulder and her hand on his chest. His heart hammered against her palm.

He brushed his lips along the outside of her ear, his teasing voice barely a whisper. "I know it's not why you came over, but it's definitely a plus."

She smiled at the gentle sensation and struggled to find her voice. "I can't believe you did that." It had never felt so good in her imagination.

He traced his fingers up her bare spine. "It seemed appropriate."

"I'm not complaining. You should trust your instinct more often."

"I'll keep that in mind." A tiny waver lined his laugh. As if he held back… again. Or she was imagining things that weren't there, when she should be falling into this moment and enjoying it as the flash in time it was.

He tightened his grip around her, and the feeling echoed in her chest, squeezing around her heart. She snuggled closer and tried to blank out her mind.

chapter thirteen

Zane struggled to bring focus to his jumbled thoughts. He trudged from the glass building, toward his truck at the back of the business-center parking lot. Another interview down.

Fuck. He wanted to yell into the wide open space. All the people coming and going might not appreciate that, and the last thing he needed was to make his situation worse.

He'd been doing great in there, as far as he could tell. Getting along with the panel of interviewers, comprised of a manager and several peers. He'd aced all the technical questions. They were a little easy, but he couldn't be picky at this point. Then the manager asked about on-the-job experience, digging for details. Zane gave them as much as he could. The way the conversation closed off after that point told him it wasn't enough.

Maybe he'd hear back from them. He doubted it. His mood shifted another notch closer to *irritated* when he saw the woman leaning against his truck. Slacks. Long legs. Black hair pulled into a tight bun. His former commanding officer… And ex-girlfriend.

A rush of images surged into his thoughts.

Plaguing. Taunting. Tormenting. Digging into his core, until the graphic images and guilt threatened to devour him. He swallowed down the memories her presence summoned, pasted a cool smile in place, and paused when he was within conversation distance. "Sabrina."

She pushed away from the truck, and gave him full salute. "You wear the suit well, Sergeant."

The formality burrowed under his calm. "What are you doing here?"

"You weren't returning my calls, so I'm trying a new approach." Her tone was pleasant and smooth. He knew the voice—it was the one she used when tried to coax something out of someone. To figure out how they ticked. To glean enough to shift the conversation in her favor.

He wasn't interested in letting that happen. "And if you track me down, say, in front of a potential employer's office, rather than at home, you figure I'll be polite. I'll rephrase my question. How did you find me here?"

"I'm a spy." A tiny smile danced on her lips, and a giggle laced her words.

A few years ago, he fell for the act. He knew better now. "I have someplace else to be."

"If you were me, how would you have found you?" Her tone went flat, and the teasing vanished.

He ticked through a mental list of the options. She might have used the same methods they did back then, when they worked together. Gotten to know a friend of his and dragged out enough information to penetrate his computer. His ego wouldn't let him believe that could slip by him. "GPS on my phone."

"See? This is child's play for you. How'd the interview go?"

He stepped around her. "Have a nice day, Captain."

"The job won't be on the table much longer."

He paused with his hand on the door of the truck. "Which is fine. My answer hasn't changed."

"Let's go somewhere and talk. Coffee, conversation, catching up… It'll be like old times."

He clenched his jaw at the fresh wave of *old times* memories. Not just the results of his actions, but the relationship he had with her. "Not interested. If this is a limited-time offer, pull it now and go find someone else. Unless there's a reason you want it to be me."

Her bitter chuckle was enough to draw his gaze, and he turned to face her again. She clucked. "Check your ego at the door, Sergeant. You're not the best. Not anymore. But you're still incredible, and your motivations go beyond cash." The word *incredible* rolled off her tongue with smooth sensuality.

He never should have gotten involved with her. "Most people know that about me."

"Fine. I'll drop the pretenses. You're not going to find better somewhere else. This position will push your limits and give you access to top-secret technology. And don't bother playing the *morals* card. We both know that's a fuzzy line for you. If you'd walk away from your unrealistic fantasy of a civilian life, you could admit you're perfect for the kind of work I'm proposing."

"I'm not." He yanked the car door open harder than he intended. "The answer's still no. Have a good afternoon."

His hand shook as he started the truck and backed out of its spot. The confrontation wasn't a big deal. A stilted conversation, at worst. Her words haunted him though. The certainty he'd cave again. That regardless of how hard he tried to convince himself he wasn't that man, her offer was more tempting than ever. Not only because he couldn't find work, but because she was right. It would push his limits. He'd gain so much experience.

He stowed his doubt under familiar reassurances. There was no reason for him to go back to that. He'd learned that lesson. The words repeated in his head as he drove home, running round and round until he believed them.

The familiar scents of paper and glass cleaner greeted Riley when she pushed into the comic store. Archer looked up from his spot across the room the moment the door chimed, and his smile grew when he saw her.

"Hey." His greeting was warm.

"Hey, yourself."

His smile wilted a little. "You're not here for me."

Guilt that it was so obvious tickled her senses. She could at least make small talk. "I didn't say that. What's up?"

He shook his head and stepped aside. "Nice try, but I'm not buying it. He's upstairs."

"Archer." She reached out but dropped her hand before it connected with him. What was she going to say? She couldn't give him false hope. An apology didn't sound appropriate, since she hadn't done anything wrong.

He stepped farther away. "No big deal. I have work to do anyway."

Relief at the quick reprieve made her guilt grow, and she wove her way through the store and toward the back stairs without much more than a quick goodbye. She should have gone through the back entrance and avoided Archer altogether, but old habits died hard.

She still struggled with feeling bad about not feeling bad for brushing Archer off when she knocked on Zane's door.

"'S open."

She pushed inside, latched the door shut behind her, and flipped the lock into place. She wasn't sure why, but something told her it might be a good idea.

Zane stood at the opposite end of the room in the kitchen area, leaning against the counter near the sink, and eating a Popsicle. He gave her an exaggerated wink. "Do anything for you, baby?"

Some of her tension evaporated at the display. She laughed and crossed the room. "Are you saying you're interested in letting me watch you lick phallic things?"

"No."

"Too bad." She pushed out her lower lip. Stepping forward, she wrapped her hand around his wrist and sucked the sweet slowly into her mouth, devouring the entire length before pulling back with a slurp. A low groan tore from his throat. She licked her lips, eyes wide and—she hoped—innocent, as she looked at him again.

He tossed the Popsicle in the sink. "You're evil. Like a hundred and twenty percent."

She stepped away, thumbs in her pockets, tugging down the waistband of her jeans. "Are you complaining?"

"Not even close." He nudged her toward the couch and nodded at the laptop on the coffee table. "Watch with me."

She dropped onto the futon next to him, her arm brushing his. "What are we watching?" She blinked and looked a second time. *He wasn't.* Really?

Thin, animated girls, with Crayola-colored hair and skirts so short they didn't even cover their asses, battled evil cartoon villains. "Why are you watching *Sailor Moon*?"

"I wanted to see something."

"The subtle lesbian subtext?" She knew a lot of people loved the show and considered it their introduction to anime—Japanese cartoons—but she'd never been able to get into it.

"Honestly…" He shifted in his seat and rested his arm on the back of the couch, his attention on her. "It's really a more in-your-face kind of thing. Also, I was thinking about how cool it would be if that were your stuff. Can you imagine them animating your drawings?"

She could. She had. "It's still an excuse."

He shrugged. "It is. I was bored. I didn't know what you'd want to watch, so I grabbed something I thought might make me laugh."

She leaned her head on his arm, enjoying the warmth of his skin against hers. "Did it work?"

"Absolutely. It's hilarious. You should try it."

She twisted her mouth. He knew how she felt about the show.

He pulled his arm away so he could turn back to the laptop screen, but settled his hand on her leg. "Give it a try, keeping in mind you're supposed to laugh."

She rested her fingers on his. Had they always been this physical and intimate, even as friends? The question came from nowhere, and she pushed it aside. "All right. I'll try."

He glanced at her. "Just remember, if any of the intense battles get to be too much, I'm here for you."

"You're such a gentleman like that."

Intense battles. Dork. Still, it gave her an idea. He let his attention drift back to the show, and she did the same. Her opportunity was coming soon. The music and creepy feeling on the screen helped the cartoon-tension build.

The moment the villain burst onto the scene, flamboyant and sparkling with black glitter, she screamed and buried her face in his chest.

He jumped. "Holy shit." His heart beat out a frantic rhythm. "You scared the crap out of me."

She laughed, face against his ribs. Warmth seeped into her ear, as she listened to his racing heart. She inhaled softly, breathing in the comforting scent of body wash and deodorant. "Sorry." She didn't sound remotely apologetic. "You sure you're not the one who needs a place to hide?"

"I'm good like this." His voice took on a husky tone, and he trailed his fingers through her hair.

She pulled away, retort catching in her throat

when she saw the way he watched her. Heat spread over her face. She adjusted her weight on the futon, turning to face him. Snippets of the day before flashed through her mind, making her body tingle. She kissed him, not resisting when he ran his hands up her arms and then held her in place by the back of her neck.

She broke away, loving the question and want in his eyes. Smirking, she trailed her finger down the side of his face. She shifted into his lap and straddled his legs. "Getting comfortable."

He moved his hands to her lower back, pulled her close, and returned the kiss, scraping her bottom lip with his teeth and not letting her go.

She pressed her chest against his, their thin tees not providing much of a barrier. His heat mingled with the brush of fabric on her nipples, and she moved against him to build the friction.

He slid his hands to her ass, making her arch her back. She broke away long enough to look him in the eye, her breath coming out in needy bursts. "We seem to be making a habit of this."

He nipped at her lower lip, and then glided his mouth down her jaw, until his lips found the hollow at the base of her neck. "It's because you're so addictive." His words vibrated against her skin.

Desire thrummed through her, leaving every nerve ending screaming for more. Heat pulsed between her legs. She didn't want to interrupt the moment, but she had to know what this was. It would be all right. He'd confirm they were still friends and give her a hint of where this was going, and they could keep making out. "For how long?"

"I don't... I mean..." He pulled away, uncertainty marring his smile.

That's not how he was supposed to respond. She went rigid. "I shouldn't have said that."

A frown slipped in to obliterate his amusement. "We're just fooling around. That was the deal."

"Yeah, of course." Her heart thudded in her chest like a rock grinding against her ribs.

"I didn't realize things had evolved. Do you want more?"

Why had she let her heart wander down this path? He was supposed to be happy about the question. Tell her he felt the same way. That she wasn't the only one falling hard and fast.

Wait. *Falling?* She knew better than to attach herself to a guy because she slept with him. "Of course not. Forget I brought it up." She extracted herself from his lap and stood in front of him.

"Riley." He grasped her fingers, holding her in place.

She stared down at him, hating the hope that surged inside and mingled with desire. Did this mean more than flirting and getting off? Would he say it?

He looked away, dropping her hand. "I don't know what to say."

Damn it. Hurt throbbed in every muscle. It really was a game to him. "It's cool. *Friends with benefits*—that's all this is." She shifted from one foot to the other, frowning deeper when she caught a glimpse of something leaning against the far wall. How had she missed that before? "Is that my sketchpad?" She grabbed her beloved book, her confusion growing.

"You kept forgetting to pick it up."

"You changed the subject when I asked for it."

"You didn't complain at the time."

Too many flavors of frustration and hurt flowed through her, for her to focus on any single one. "And I'm not now. Except, you know, for the whole distracting-me thing. Speaking of which, we're talking about my sketchpad, not the ways you distracted me from it."

"Is this how it usually happens? You hide how you really feel, until you spill it all at once, and then expect the guy to respond immediately, or you take it all back? Is this what happened last time?"

How dare he throw Archer or anyone else back in her face? After everything she told him in confidence, the accusation stung like lemon juice in an open wound. "You really think that little of me?"

"That's not what I meant."

"I'm not the one who hasn't dared get close to someone since his fiancée left him. Oh, wait, and the Air Force girlfriend you loved so much, whom you never mention. Ever."

"Because your track record with men is so fantastic." His tone was flat.

She felt like she'd been socked in the gut with every concern she had about her love life, everything she hoped no one else saw, but knew they did. "Why are you doing this?"

He met her toe-to-toe, something new flashing in his eyes. "Maybe I'm trying to piss you off."

She choked on a response as a fresh wash of hurt seeped into her. "Excuse me?"

"*Maybe*"—his tone was snide, but pain still

filled his eyes—"I'm trying to push you away." As the words tumbled past his lips, he worked his jaw up and down and frowned. "Pissing you off and letting you make the decision to leave is a lot easier than telling you to go."

She swallowed the pang in her throat. "Why do you want me gone?"

"Because you deserve better, Riley. We're walking this impossible line, pretending the sex is just physical, ignoring that we've never been *just friends*, and you need more than I can give you."

Whatever she'd expected, it wasn't that. But when she thought about it, he'd been dropping the hints all along. "Why are you so convinced you don't deserve me?"

His laugh was bitter and choked as he scrubbed his hand over the stubble on the top of his head. "You think I'm this good, kind person, and I'm not."

"Why not? Is it because of what your granddad said? I know you love the man, but he's not right about that. You're not evil. What the hell does that even mean?"

He sank on the edge of the futon, clenching and loosening a fist. His hand shook. "I didn't turn down the surveillance job when I found out what I was doing. I didn't walk away in some huff of indignation, spouting bullshit about moral gray areas. I stayed."

Riley knew there was more, but he wasn't giving her enough to figure out what made that so bad. "You were military, and it was your job."

"No." He dropped his head into his hands and dragged in a stuttered breath. "They gave me an out.

Told me I could be transferred. Go do something else. I liked the challenge. Okay, sure, I was violating a few people's privacy." He tightened his jaw and flared his nostrils. "But I'm not stupid. If it wasn't me, it would be someone else, and I was pushing my boundaries—doing things I'd never done before. I could make all the excuses in the world for why I stayed, but that was what it came down to."

Acid churned in her gut, and she bit the inside of her cheek to keep from saying something she hadn't thought out. "But you left eventually, right?"

"Yeah." He was turned in her direction, but he didn't see her. "I did. When I saw the first news stories, I ignored them. Hidden headlines in local papers, about a couple of the people we'd gathered intel on. Their deaths. The accidents. The car crash, or boating trip gone wrong, that took them and their entire family."

She leaned her arm on the table, to support herself. "That doesn't mean it was your fault."

"It was. I looked deeper after the third accident. Found hints our information led to the decision. I asked Sabrina about it, and she confirmed. What we'd helped uncover took those people out of the picture."

Numbness filled Riley. "It's not like you pulled the trigger."

"I might as well have." He finally focused on her again. "Entire families died because I wanted to be challenged. I found that information. I dug until it happened. That's why I don't deserve you. That's why you need to leave."

She opened her mouth, but words failed her.

"I don't want you here, Riley." His voice took on a hard edge. "I don't want you in my life. *We* don't mean anything. What we did was just sex. Me being selfish. Using you."

"Bullshit." She still didn't know what to do with his confession, but he couldn't take this from her. "I knew what I was doing. I wanted the sex. I want you."

"You think that, but it's not true. Let's be honest. You don't know what you want." The waver in his gaze and the way he turned away as he spoke told her he didn't believe his own words.

That didn't stop them from burrowing under her skin and gnawing at her frayed threads of composure. "You don't really think that."

A pause dragged between them, before he said, "Of course I do. No one knows you better than me. It doesn't matter if I think you're awesome or amazing, you don't believe it, and your opinion of you is all that matters. Go home. Don't call me again. Find someone else to fuck with your life."

"Zane."

"*Leave.*"

She wanted to argue, but the strength wasn't there. This was too much at once. She couldn't process anything but how intensely it all hurt. She spun away without another word. It took the last of her restraint to hold back the torrent of tears as she stormed from the room. At least she didn't pass Archer anywhere between the apartment and the back door. She couldn't have handled the most basic human interaction just then.

She made it to her car and collapsed in the front

seat before the tears took over. Sobs wracked her body, and she hugged herself tight, trying to keep from shaking apart. She leaned her forehead on the steering wheel, grateful for the cool morning. Every inch of her psyche hurt. Zane's words echoed in her head, gnawing at every insecurity she had. And then his confession—what was she supposed to do with that? Too many questions assaulted her for her to focus on anything.

On top of it all, instead of telling him she didn't hold his actions against him, instead of staying and comforting him like she always promised she'd do, she'd wrapped self-pity around her and left. He carried this massive burden, and she was in her car, crying because he knew the same truth about her that everyone else did.

But she couldn't go back and apologize. He didn't want her there, and she didn't know if she was strong enough to argue.

What was she supposed to do? No experience in her entire life gave her a hint for how to handle something like this.

chapter fourteen

Disgust and nausea rolled through Zane. He thought maybe sleeping, putting yesterday behind him, would make it go away. Convince him he was right to push Riley away last night. He was wrong. He told her the truth—finally spilled his big secret—and just like he expected, she left.

You told her to.

She could have argued. Could have stayed.

Do you blame her for going?

No. It was what he wanted. What was best for her. He couldn't draw her into this sinking pit with him. He was being selfish, leading her on, keeping her around, when he couldn't give her what she needed long term.

A painfully loud knock jarred him out of his own head. He could ignore it. If it was Archer, Zane didn't want to see him. Or maybe, a distraction would help him ignore his invisible wounds a bit longer.

His thoughts stalled when he yanked open the door and saw Riley. She stared at him, looking incredible despite the dark circles under her eyes and the oversized T-shirt and sweats.

He steeled himself and dragged up the resolve to push her away. It all evaporated the moment he opened his mouth. "Hey. I'm making coffee. Do you want some?"

She shook her head and stepped around him. Would she sit? Stay a while? That seemed like a horrible idea, but it sounded so good.

She lingered in the middle of the room, rubbed her face, and looked at him again. "I don't know why I'm here; you made yourself clear yesterday. But I still can't leave this alone."

"Can you forgive me for what I did? For who I am?" He had no right to ask her that. He couldn't forgive himself.

She looked drained. Her shoulders drooped when she flopped to sit on the edge of the futon. She moved her lips a few times, before finally saying, "I don't know."

"Then we're done here."

"You misunderstand." Exhaustion lined her words. "I can see how much this devours you—what happened overseas. I don't hold that against you. It's going to take time for me to process; I'll be honest. I don't think any less of you, though. I still adore you."

"Then what's the problem?" He shouldn't ask. He didn't want to know.

"You don't trust me. Which is your right, but if we don't have that, we don't have anything. It's my fault, too. This whole friends-with-benefits thing was a bad idea."

Damn straight. So why did hearing it gnaw deeper into his senses? Plenty of other women made cutoffs look erotic and tasted like cherry lip-gloss. "I still don't know why you're here," he said.

She nodded at the empty space next to her. He sat, and she twisted to face him, legs crossed. A heavy pause spread through the room, before she finally spoke. "High school. Senior year."

The four words echoed in his thoughts, and he froze. He forced himself to relax. At least if their past was going to torment them, they'd go full-throttle. There were so many old scars there. "You want to rehash what was some really miserable shit for both of us?"

"Homecoming."

"Don't do this." He dropped his gaze. Of course she wanted to talk about that. She was going to push until she reopened more wounds.

"I'd been hinting all summer that I wanted to you ask me."

The revelation dug deep. Why did she say that now? Why not ten years ago? It didn't matter. He'd already dealt with that and moved on. So much had happened since, that moment shouldn't even be a blip on his radar any longer. "To homecoming?"

"Yes."

"So why didn't you ask me? An even better question is, why did you say *yes* to someone else?"

Her frown deepened. "I was an insecure teenage girl, with dreams of you being Prince Charming. I said *yes* to someone else, because I was hoping it would catch your attention and you would see what you were missing and ask me yourself."

"You did it to make me jealous?" he asked in disbelief. Such a childish game. So why did it tug at something warm inside?

"Insecure teenage girl, remember?"

A laugh slipped out at the confession. Was he actually starting to relax? This easy banter with her was what soothed him and kept him from slipping into his own regrets. Even when they hit a painful subject, if they could move past it, it comforted him. He didn't want that. Hadn't earned the right to move on.

As long as they were confessing, he might as well spill it all. "I'd been trying to work up the courage to ask you for weeks. When someone asked me that morning, I told her *no* and realized I needed to suck it up and let you know how I felt. Except you already had a date. I pretended to be happy for you, because that's what best friends do, and I didn't want you to think I was a bad sport. I convinced myself I read your hints wrong and we really were just friends. So I went back to her and told her I'd love to go with her if she'd still have me."

She stared back, silent.

"What are you thinking?"

Her smile looked forced. "Just wondering how things would have been different if we'd hooked up back then."

"We'd be miserable." That's why he brought it up. For as many times as he had the same what-if thought, he already knew the answer.

"Why do you say that?" she asked.

She wasn't supposed to question him. He had his reasons. "You don't feel that way about me. Imagine if we'd indulged a temporary crush and broken up. We wouldn't be here now." Not that he knew where *here* was.

Hurt echoed in her eyes. "I guess."

He hated the distance between them and that it grew with every passing second. He hated even worse that he was the current source of her gloom. "We didn't belong together then, and we don't belong together now." He shouldn't have let things go this far. It had been stupid and shortsighted. Destroying what they had, because he was thinking with his dick.

"Do you really feel that way?" She clenched her jaw and narrowed her eyes.

"Of course I do." Part of him whispered it was a lie, but a louder voice screamed nothing had ever been truer. "That's the way it is."

"I see." She stood, not looking at him. "I don't know what I'm doing here, then."

"Me neither." He forced his hands to stay by his side. Swallowed his call to stop her from walking out the door. This was the way it had to be.

chapter fifteen

Riley leaned over the butcher-block countertop, calligraphy pen poised over a place card, waiting for Kenzie to spell out another name. They were seated across from each other on the tall stools bordering the breakfast bar.

Creating the place cards for her sister's wedding reception should be a distraction, but Kenzie wanted to write them all up, in order to seat all the right people by all the other right people. Every time there was a lull while Kenzie searched for the next name, Riley's thoughts took over again, dragging her into the frustration and lack of answers that had tormented her since Zane forced her out of his life a few days ago.

Kenzie gave her the next name, and Riley let the letters flow in black script across the card. She blew on the ink for a few seconds, to make sure it dried, and then handed it over.

"You're quiet tonight." Kenzie's attention never left her list of guest names.

"I guess." Riley didn't want to talk about it. Rather, the person she wanted to talk about it with was the source of her angst. She *knew* he didn't want to bring their friendship to an end, hated the idea as much as she did, and yet he let his past torment him into thinking he didn't have a choice. Except, every time she honed in on the thought, doubt told her she read the situation wrong. Again. Like she had with every other guy she knew, but with Zane, the consequences were more serious. It wasn't as simple as a broken heart. His hurt ran deeper.

"No, Stephen with a *ph*." Kenzie placed a hand over Riley's and pulled the misspelled card away.

"Sorry." Riley sighed and grabbed another piece of decorated stock to write on. She'd lost count of how many times she screwed up that night. She was positive Kenzie knew the exact number, but her sister was kind enough not to call her on it.

Riley should make another effort to make this right with Zane. Make it clear she was taking the sex off the table, and was there for him. But if he pushed her away another time, how many *no*s would it take for her to get the hint?

"Okay. Just stop." Kenzie plucked the pen from her hand and capped it. "Stephen also doesn't have a Z. Or an A. Though at least you got the N and E right."

Heat flooded Riley's cheeks. She hadn't quite written Zane's name; it was some sort of bizarre hybrid of jumbled letters. "Sorry."

"Do you want to talk about it?" Kenzie studied her, concern heavy in her face.

Yes. "I'll be fine."

Kenzie shook her head. "Sure." She slid another card across the counter. "Keep in mind I only picked up so many of these things."

"I get it. Stephen then?"

"No. I want him sitting somewhere else." Kenzie paused longer than she should have. "Archer Yates."

Riley's hand froze around the pen, gripping it until her knuckles ached, but unable to let go. "You did that on purpose."

Kenzie stared back, her face an impassive mask. "You think I'd put my entire reception in disarray, to squeeze information out of you that you don't want to give me? He's Jen's plus one. I want them at this table."

Riley clenched her jaw. She knew Archer and his sister were attending, had even assured Kenzie several times she was fine with it, but it wasn't as if she was going to argue. Kenzie and Jen were friends, and it wasn't Riley's place to ruin her sister's wedding plans.

"I'm sorry." Riley forced her hand to remain steady while she inked in his name. "Except this doesn't put them at the same table, because there's only one spot left, and you haven't split up any of your other guests."

Kenzie flinched. "This is different. They're not a couple. They should mingle."

Riley stared back, her mouth twisted in disbelief. "You're going to break your own rules? Willingly?"

"What?" Kenzie took the card from her but didn't place it on top of the stack, as she had all the others. "My rules, my exceptions."

Kenzie didn't make exceptions. Riley pursed her lips. "Sure."

"Fine." Kenzie's shoulders slumped. "What's the deal with you and Zane?"

The deal was she'd made the same mistake she had with Archer—slept with a good friend and confused sex with love. Except it wasn't that simple, and this wasn't really about her. Not directly. The deal was she felt more helpless than she ever remembered feeling in her life. She dropped her pen. "I'm done."

"Riley."

Riley's gut turned in on itself. "Nothing." The single word came out harsher than she expected. "There's no *deal* with us."

"You were holding hands half the night at dinner."

The memory throbbed in Riley's temple, and an ache settled in her throat. She couldn't find a response, not that she trusted herself to speak anyway. Silence stretched between them.

"I'll drop it." Kenzie turned her attention to the already scripted name cards, straightening and over-straightening them.

"We're sleeping together." The words tumbled past Riley's lips before she could figure out if she wanted to stop them or not. It made her ill to have that out there, but at the same time, it was a relief.

"You should have told me you guys were dating. That's…" Kenzie trailed off, smile vanishing. "You're not dating."

Riley shook her head. "It wasn't supposed to be this way. We had some fun while he was deployed. You know. Talking and *stuff*. When he got back, we agreed it might be even more fun to fool around in person. We promised we could stay friends. Except now I'm falling for him, and I know I wasn't supposed to, and what if I spend the rest of my life unable to tell when I care about someone and when I'm just lonely?"

That wasn't actually the problem. Not by a long shot. But she didn't know how to explain the reality to her sister, and Zane's story wasn't her secret to share.

Kenzie covered Riley's hand again, her tone soft. "You're wrong."

Riley's insides threatened to fold in half. She couldn't hide her hurt. "I didn't mean to."

"That's not what I mean," Kenzie said quickly. "I mean you're wrong about not being able to tell the difference."

"You're sweet, but I'm not." Riley couldn't swallow. Her throat was too dry and raw from hidden tears.

"Why would you say that? You were the one who told me you wanted that shared look. That respect. That admiration. You have all that and more with Zane."

Riley hated herself for clinging to the words. False hope would set her up for more heartache, but she couldn't ignore it. "You think?"

"Would I say it if I didn't believe it?"

Good point. Her sister was diplomatic, but she never outright made things up. "I guess not, but it doesn't matter, if he doesn't feel the same."

"Sorry to interrupt, ladies." Scott appeared behind Kenzie. He rested his hand at the small of her back. "Caterer is on the phone. Will you talk to him?"

Kenzie rolled her eyes. "You can't handle it?"

The corner of Scott's mouth pulled up in a smirk. "I'm about thirty seconds from telling him exactly what I think of his phony French accent and completely inauthentic food."

"Fine." Kenzie's grin defied the irritation in her voice. She looked at Riley. "I'll be right back, and we'll figure it out." She kissed Scott, lingering for a few seconds before pulling away.

Damn it, Riley *did* want that. And she wanted it with Zane. She didn't hold his past against him; she only wanted to help him through it. To see him whole again. She dropped her chin into her palm, gaze locked on the countertop. This was such a mess.

The leather on the stool next to her creaked when Scott sat down. "So, this boyfriend of yours…"

Swell. Nine times out of ten, she adored Scott. Right then, she was so very not in the mood for his brand of… *him.* "He's not my boyfriend."

"Sorry." He sounded anything but. "This guy you know. Zane, right?"

She glared at the countertop. "What about him?"

Scott grabbed a stack of name cards from the middle of the group, flipping through them, but not reordering them. "Kenzie says he was electronic surveillance in the Air Force for six years."

God, this was so far from a conversation she wanted to have. "So?"

"Is he any good?"

Riley finally turned her attention to Scott, looking for any hint of what was going on. Scott's expression was the same as always. Smiling, a little arrogant, unassuming.

"He's the best," she said. It didn't matter what Zane thought of himself, his skills were top notch. "He'd probably hate me for telling you this"—*if he doesn't already*—"but so many people already know, it's not like it's a big secret. Before he enlisted, he got really good at finding holes in company websites. He never did anything like on the scale of a chaos hacker, but he did manage to snag a couple of games before they were released. He's only gotten better since."

Scott's expression flickered for a moment between surprised, pleased, and irritated before returning to normal. "Where's he working now?"

She paused, not comfortable spilling that kind of information, and still having no idea why Scott cared. "He's between contracts. Looking for a company that will challenge him and know how to utilize his skills. Things like that."

"So he's unemployed."

Riley sighed. "Is this going somewhere?"

"You know one of the things I love about Kenzie?"

Riley was caught off guard by the rapid change in subject. Listening to her sister's love-struck fiancé sing Kenzie's praises wouldn't help her mood. "She's got a nice ass?"

"She's not you."

The three words hit Riley hard.

"I'm not done," Scott said.

She nodded, not able to ignore the sting in her eyes.

"It's what I adore about you too, baby sister. She's a brilliant, organized mind, and you're intelligent and creative, and anyone who thinks she should be more like you or you should be more like her is missing something significant."

Her hurt vanished. She opened her mouth to thank him for the compliment, but he talked over her. "That includes you."

"Hey. I'm back," Kenzie said.

Scott was on his feet again in an instant. He wrapped an arm around Kenzie's waist, dipped her, and swallowed her laugh with a deep kiss.

"What do you mean?" Riley asked, once her sister was upright again, trying to squelch the pang that wished she could have the easy fun and obvious affection they did.

Scott kissed her on the cheek. "Ask Zane. He knows." With that, he was gone, vanished back into the living room or wherever he was hiding.

"What was that about?" Kenzie dropped back into her seat.

Riley shook her head. Scott was bizarrely cryptic sometimes, she suspected because he didn't think the same way as most people, not as an attempt to be obtuse. Even if she couldn't translate the conversation, it cemented for her the need to approach Zane at least one more time.

"Anyway…" Kenzie frowned when she saw a stack of name cards out of line, and squared them all up again before setting them back in their proper spot. "Whatever you decide about Zane, keep in mind that the rift is already there. It's obvious. Repair it or lose him."

Riley let the words roll around in her head. It sounded so simple. *Repair it or lose him.* If only it were that easy.

chapter sixteen

Zane was on his feet in an instant at the knock on the door. He growled at his anticipation. He didn't want it to be Riley, regardless of what the hollow pit behind his ribs insisted.

His heart sank against his will when he saw who it was. He didn't bother with a smile as he yanked the door open. He wasn't in the mood for Sabrina. Her dark brown hair was pulled into a thick braid that draped her shoulder, drawing the eye to a low-cut T-shirt that toed the line between too tight and just right. Regardless of how much he didn't want to see her, he still couldn't defy propriety. He kept his attention on her face. "Can I help you?"

Sabrina lounged against the doorframe, a smirk dancing on full, too-red lips. She stepped closer, nudging him with her frame. "Invite me in?"

Fuck. He hadn't seen this behavior since they were first assigned to work together. Back then, his dick controlled the conversations when she did this. Today, he wasn't in the mood. He put more distance between them. "Do you want to sit?"

She ducked her head and looked up at him through heavy black lashes. "Only if you're the seat."

He didn't try to hide his irritation. "There's no need, really. I'm standing, so there's plenty of room on the couch."

She traced a finger along the edge of her T-shirt, pausing at her cleavage. "It looks lonely over there."

He pinched the bridge of his nose. "What do you want?"

"You."

"No, really."

She crossed her arms, pushing her tits together and up. "So blondes are more your thing?"

His veins filled with ice. She knew about Riley. "Can't say I have a preference."

"You know what I do for a living, right?" Sabrina raised an eyebrow, studying him with disbelief.

Zane struggled to hold back his creeping dread. "She was a friend before I deployed. That's all."

"Really?" Her laugh chilled him further. "Okay. Let's play this game. *Please, Ms. Spy, leave her out of this. She doesn't know. It doesn't have anything to do with her.*"

Zane clenched his jaw and his fists, and let a growl escape her chest. "So you're here to... threaten the people I know? That won't end well for you."

"Oh, so cute. But that's not your line. Now you say, *I'll do anything you want. Just leave them alone.*"

He took a step toward her, and then another, twisted satisfaction growing inside when she moved back. "No." He kept his voice low and even. "Now I tell you, if you're here to threaten me—directly or otherwise—you won't like the results. I can destroy you digitally, and you know it."

"There's the man I adore." Her smile unnerved him more than the innuendo about Riley. "I'm not here to threaten anyone. Nothing bad is going to happen to your playmate. We don't work like that."

"You work *exactly* like that."

She shrugged. "Busted. But not when it comes to her. She's a blip. Doesn't know anything. Doesn't mean anything. Which is why I don't understand your infatuation with her. What are you doing, Sergeant? Playing house? Pretending you're normal? Convincing yourself this lifestyle is going to make you happy? I'm not threatening you, because we both know torture doesn't work. Especially long term. This is motivation. You want this job. You were made for this type of work."

He tried to hide his cringe at how close to home her words hit. "You need to leave."

She stood her ground. "You come work with me again, and it's not about clinging to some past that was never real—unlike the life you're trying to live now. I don't care that you were an okay lay. Though, God, some of the emails the two of you shared… Wow, she thinks you're all that."

He should have known his exchanges with Riley weren't private. "This conversation is over."

"Ditch the blonde, come work for us. The money is good. You'll never stop growing. Right now, you're just a hack who can't keep up. And really, do you think she's going to want you once she figures out who you are? We already know, and that's why you're so valuable to us."

"*Get out*." Zane couldn't find more words in the midst of his anger.

"Sergeant Petrov." Her voice was gentle. Coaxing. Condescending. "You're going to regret this"—she finally reached for the doorknob—"but I won't ask again." She didn't wait for a response but slipped out and tugged the door shut behind her.

Zane sank back against a nearby wall, shaking with anger and trying to ignore the thread of creeping sick about the exchange. Riley might not mean anything to the CIA, but she was his world.

He'd do absolutely anything for her, including making sure she ended up with a good guy. Someone who wasn't him. He didn't think he could ever atone for his sins, but if it was possible, he'd start here.

Riley could do this. She could talk to Zane, figure out what was going on, and convince him she was there for him. She repeated the reassurances, trying to make herself believe them. Relief and nausea flooded her when she saw Zane's car. So he was home. *Good. Perfect. Right?*

She swallowed the sickness climbing inside her and headed toward the back stairs that led to his apartment. Her step faltered when she saw an unfamiliar woman walking down. The brunette's cheeks were flushed, and a smile stretched her face the moment she made eye contact with Riley.

The stranger came to a stop in front of her, her smile too big to be genuine. "You must be Riley. I'm

Sabrina. I've heard so much about you."

The Air Force girlfriend. The commanding officer who'd been by Zane's side through this entire mess. Riley pushed back every single trace of revulsion, holding on to it for later. "Same. I can't say any of it was good, though." She didn't care cattiness filled her retort.

"I hope I didn't spoil him for you." Sabrina's grin spread. "I think they heard me screaming his name in pleasure in the shop. God, he gets so rough when he's turned on. Yanking my hair. Forcing me down. That man is incredible when he lets himself off his leash."

Riley's convictions fled. A series of childish retorts rolled through her thoughts, but she couldn't find any real, tangible response. Sabrina brushed past her with a smirk, and Riley turned, held up her hand, middle finger extended.

It didn't matter if what Sabrina implied was true. Riley was here to resurrect her friendship with Zane. If sex was out of the equation, that was fine, but she wouldn't share him. Not like that. She forced one foot in front of the other until she stood before his apartment. It took every last ounce of willpower to raise her hand and knock.

Seconds later, the door was flung open, startling her. She stepped back at the fury on Zane's face, doubt growing when his expression instantly melted into a tiny smile.

"Hey." His voice was low. He stepped aside. "Come on in."

Confusion throbbed in her temple, as she stepped around him. "It's not a bad time?"

"No." He closed the door behind her but hovered near it. "I'm surprised you're here."

Judging from his expression, whatever happened with Sabrina didn't leave him as satisfied as it did her. Good to know. Riley faltered, not finding her next reply. Damn, this was awkward. "I told myself I'd do this one more time, now we've both had a few days to think. But I won't be back every two days, begging for you to hear me out, if you're not interested." She loved him, though she didn't know what kind of love it was. She wouldn't be anyone's emotional punching bag.

"I understand." He reached for her, but dropped his hand at the last second.

The foot between them felt like a mile. Riley grabbed her left arm with her right hand. "I just met Sabrina."

The fury was on his face again for the briefest moment before it vanished and he turned his attention to the ceiling. "How'd that go?"

Riley shrugged, not trusting herself to say much. "Openly hostile. What did you two get up to?"

"Same things as always." He didn't hide his irritation so well that time.

A whimper rose in her throat, and she choked it back. He didn't want her asking about it. That was fine; she could do that. Not that it was appropriate for her to ask whom he was sleeping with. She nodded toward the futon. "Can we talk?"

"Sure."

The moment she was inside, he kicked the door shut behind her. A strange uncertainty and something she'd never seen before hid behind his look. "I really wondered if I'd see you again."

She clenched her jaw, unsure how to respond. His uncertainty added to hers, making it difficult to collect her thoughts.

"I…" He furrowed his brow and clenched his hands into fists. He took a deep breath, then another and another. His frame relaxed. He looked at her again, a new clarity in his expression. Resting his hands on both sides of her face, he pressed his lips softly to hers.

The whimper she'd been trying to hold back escaped at the tender gesture. She closed her eyes and sank into the kiss, heart hammering against her ribcage. How had she ever doubted this was anything other than electric? She pressed closer, wanting to feel all of him.

He slid his hands down her arms, raising goose bumps everywhere he touched, and rested them on her hips. He traced a slow line along her jaw to her neck with his lips, and she tilted her head back, lost in the sensation.

He pushed the bottom of her T-shirt up and rested his palms on her bare waist. Was this his way of distracting her? Turning any chance at conversation into sex, so he had an excuse to kick her out again when it was over?

She wanted him so desperately, but not if she wasn't the only one. Not this time. Not with him. She covered his hands with hers and pushed him away. "Not tonight."

He stepped back, hurt mingling with that something she still hadn't identified in his expression. "Of course not. I shouldn't have assumed."

She forced a smile. "It's not that." She fumbled for the right words. The best way to tell him why she was here. Nothing came to mind though. Frustration welled inside. What now?

chapter seventeen

Zane beat back his aggravation. Of course. He'd tried to cross that line one too many times with her, and she was getting tired of it. The realization pulsed through him, and he tried to grab any lingering emotion from inside, wrap it in a ball, and tuck it away in the bottom of his gut. "What is it, then?"

She perched on the edge of the futon he'd never folded back into a couch the night before. She was several feet away, ankles crossed and knees tucked to the side. "I was hoping we could just hang out."

"Watch movies or something?"

She shrugged. "Or talk or something."

Like they used to do back in high school. When they both pretended they didn't have a crush on each other, and neither of them knew it. He didn't miss those days. Except maybe the bits when she fell asleep in his bed. That was always nice. Though it had been innocent, he'd loved being able to curl around her like they were the only two people in the world.

He pushed the thought away. Childish fantasy. He dropped onto the opposite edge of the futon from her, the battered quilt wrinkling under him. "I can do that. How's your sister?"

There. That was neutral, right? So why did she look like she swallowed a mouthful of bad milk?

"She's good. Great. I think she's the kind of person who was made to get married. I'm pretty certain this whole planning thing is just one orgasm after another for her." She clamped her jaw shut. "I mean... You know what I mean."

"I do."

She fidgeted. "I'm going to try this one more time and hope I make myself clear. Whatever happened while you were gone, it doesn't change what I think of you or how I feel about you. I know who you are, even if you can't see it. I'm not going to run away because you made mistakes. I'll leave— walk out of your life for good—if that's what you want. But don't you dare push me away because you think that's what's best for me. That's my decision to make, not yours."

The words struck a chord he didn't want to acknowledge. He couldn't have this conversation with her. Not now, maybe not ever. The high-school memory popped back into his thoughts, and he was about to ignore it when inspiration struck. That memory was exactly what he needed. "Do you want to sleep over?"

"Zane."

He ignored the pleading in her voice. "Like we used to. Except this time we don't pretend we fell asleep on accident. Stay over. We'll be careless kids. We'll have a sleepover, pop popcorn, and watch the stupidest movies ever. The ones we loved back then."

A smile crept onto her face. Sadness tinged it, but it was a start. "Did you hear anything I said?"

"All of it."

"Are you going to respond?"

"Give me time." He tried to hide his wince as soon as the words passed his lips. Had he let too much of himself show?

Something flickered in her eyes, but it was gone before he could interpret it. She bounced to her feet, false cheer flooding in. "All right. I'm in."

This was what they needed. Teasing. Joking. Fun. It was what they were missing. Even if her actions did look forced and mechanical. That would pass.

She bent at the waist to flip through a list of films on his hard drive. "What do we watch first?"

"Whatever you want."

She double-clicked on *Bill and Ted's Excellent Adventure*. He shouldn't have been surprised. They'd watched that movie to death when they were younger, each of them taking one of the lead characters' lines. "You know, I kind of miss that old black-and-white TV of yours," she said as the movie started rolling.

"I kind of don't." He much preferred the widescreen multi-media laptop he'd gotten as a *welcome back* gift. It didn't have the horsepower he needed for some of his extracurricular activities, but since he had more or less outgrown hacking websites—and didn't miss it nearly as much as Sabrina thought—he wasn't too concerned about it.

She pushed him back on the futon as the movie started. "Get comfortable."

He shifted his weight until his back was against the wall, legs out in front of him. His cock throbbed when she crawled over the blanket toward him. The sitting-in-his-lap thing was new, since he'd gotten back.

"I swear"—she pushed his legs apart, to sit between them—"if I feel something hard poking me in the butt…"

She would. There was absolutely no way around that. "You'll know I'm a healthy man and you're an incredibly sexy woman, sitting as close as is physically possible?"

She pulled his arms around her waist. "I was going to say I'd be flattered, but you win."

He wanted to strip off her clothes and watch her squirm and moan in pleasure, instead of paying attention to the movie. But this was nice too. Actually, when he thought about it, this was amazing. Maybe it was a bad idea.

"When did it happen?" Riley's voice was soft, as she leaned more of her weight against his chest.

The almost overwhelming desire to spend the night making love to her? He was starting to think it had always been there. "When did what happen?"

"When did we lose this? The ability to let loose with each other. Things have been strained for so long. I mean, not like in a way most people would notice, but I see it, and I'm pretty sure you do too. Those awkward pauses that never used to be there. Did it happen when you enlisted?"

The answer popped into his head, and he realized he'd been thinking about it for a long time yet never recognized it. "It happened when I started dating Amanda."

She leaned her head back on his shoulder, touching her cheek to his. "How do you figure?"

He expected the memories to hurt. He hadn't been down this road willingly in so long. "She hated me spending time with you."

"Why?"

"Really?"

"Yes, really."

"She was insanely jealous of you. Vocally. Intensely." Zane had never understood why, until now.

"She was insane. It's not the same. I'm still not getting it."

Because Amanda was just the girl he'd been fucking. Riley was the entire other half of his universe. "I couldn't talk to her the way I talk to you. I tried a couple times. I guess it felt like… I was betraying you."

She closed her eyes, a soft smile playing on her lips. "You were together for so long."

It was true. "She asked me to marry her, not the other way around."

Riley sat up and turned to look at him in shock. "Seriously?"

"There was always something missing there. I think she hoped marriage would fix it." The same thing Archer had said.

Riley shook her head. "It doesn't work that way."

"I know that now, but back then… Let me put it this way—why did you think people were going to hate you when they found out you turned Archer down?"

Suddenly her body wasn't molded to his anymore. Her spine went rigid. "At least one person does."

He moved a hand to the back of Riley's neck, to rub lightly. "Their opinions aren't worth shit." She relaxed under the attention. Or maybe it was the words. He wasn't sure. "That's my point. It's what we're told people do. Right? They date for a while, and as long as they get along, they get married. Everyone expects it. She and I had been together for years. I figured it was the next step."

Riley leaned back into him again. "Except there was something missing." He didn't know if she was talking about him and Amanda or her and Archer. "Getting along, nice qualities… they don't really mean anything if the two of you don't click. I mean, maybe I'm just a cynical romantic, but I'd rather go without, than tie myself to someone I don't have that spark with."

He wrapped his arms around her waist again and rested his cheek against hers. "Yeah, me too."

"About Sabrina…" She trailed off.

Where had that come from? He tried to keep his tone light and his posture casual. "What about her?"

"I guess it's none of my business, and I probably don't want to know the answer, but since I'm wondering and we're being open, I'm going to ask anyway."

He frowned, glad she couldn't see it. What was she getting at?

She shuddered. "Do you have a similar agreement with her that you do with me?"

The line of conversation made less and less sense the deeper it dove. "I don't have anything with her, let alone something even close to what you and I have." Speaking the words sent a sharp spike of heat through him. They hit so close to home, and at the same time seemed woefully inadequate to the love he had for Riley.

"So this afternoon was just a tumble because you were bored?"

It took him a moment to process what she said, and when he did, he almost choked. "This afternoon was her telling me I was stupid for turning down the CIA job. There was no *tumble*. Did she tell you that?"

"Yes." Riley's answer was almost lost among the exaggerated *boguses* in the background.

That explained why Riley seemed removed and on edge. Or he hoped it did. "I swear on all I hold dear, I haven't done anything with her or even thought about it for ages."

She sagged against him, but her neck was still straight, rigid. "The guy who fantasizes about every attractive woman he knows isn't even thinking about *it* in regards to *her*."

A smile leaked out at the dry teasing. "Most guys do that. Besides, not every woman—just you and a couple of movie stars, and honestly… really only you since we started fooling around."

"I have a hard time buying that."

He brushed his lips over the outside edge of her ear. Relief flooded him when she sighed and relaxed further instead of pulling away. "You can be a pretty all-consuming thought. I mean that in the best way possible."

When she shifted her weight and rubbed her back against him, it called to the lust he'd tried to beat back since she turned him down. Apparently his dick wasn't listening.

She trailed her fingers lightly down his forearms and then back up again. "You're just saying that to get laid."

A small laugh shook his frame. "I'm saying it because it's true." His mouth hovered millimeters from the curve where her neck met her shoulder, the soft melon scent of her shampoo searing his veins with need. Maybe this was what he needed, to let go. Guilt and regret surged back, taunting him, reminding him he hadn't earned that privilege.

chapter eighteen

Riley pressed into the warm body behind her as consciousness seeped in, burning into her memory the feeling of his chest against her back. The night before had been incredible—talking like they hadn't talked in ages. He skirted the one topic she knew lived at the forefront of his mind, but they'd get to that when he was ready.

And then falling asleep in his arms… When she climbed into his lap, she had worried it was too much. That it would take them to places it would hurt to go.

It had been worth the risk.

His warm breath tickled her neck in a steady rhythm. He was still asleep. Wake him up or bask in the comfort a little longer?

She crawled out from under his arm and blankets, and scooted to the edge of the futon. The night before had been fun, but she was still lying to herself about something important. Pretending she didn't love him intensely, and then diving into an illusion of *just friends* to get closer wasn't going to work.

Her drifting attention landed on a familiar

business card, and she tugged it from its spot on the coffee table. Had he ever called Scott? So much had happened lately. She should have asked sooner.

She plucked a ballpoint pen from a cup to the right of the computer and flipped the card over. The pen slid smoothly over the stock, and the lines filled in quickly as she sketched. Within a couple of minutes, a picture of Zane looked back at her. It was different from her comics. He was hunched over a laptop, but she'd left out the cartoony lines, giving him a more realistic appearance instead.

Her phone buzzed at her from its spot on the table, where she'd left it the night before. Out of habit, she grabbed it to scan the new email message. Questions about Zane—what to do, how to do it, how she would cope if he didn't feel the same—swirled in dizzying circles in her head.

Moving on autopilot, she pulled up her email.

Tell him and risk losing it all, or keep it to herself and risk driving herself insane with regret, because she never asked?

She paused, thumb hovering over the screen, when a familiar name caught her attention. They'd been number one on her list of agents to contact about her graphic novel. Why were they emailing her?

She needed to calm down. It was a bizarre coincidence. The knot growing in her stomach needed to go away. She clicked the message open, sickness filling her as she read.

Ms. Carter,

Thanks so much for contacting me about your book project. While the concept was unique and interesting, I felt like the artwork lacked polish. Please keep in mind this industry is subjective and...

Her vision blurred, and the words trailed off. Zane stirred behind her. She hadn't sent her work to anyone. How did she get rejected without querying?

Her artwork lacked polish?

"Hey." Sleep lined Zane's greeting.

She didn't look up. Holy hell, this hurt. Part of her knew rejection was inevitable, but she hadn't even been able to bring it on herself. How had this happened?

"Shit, Riley. What's wrong?" The bed rustled some more, and seconds later, Zane knelt in front of her. He brushed a thumb over her cheek. "Talk to me?"

Her throat was raw, and she couldn't make her voice work.

"Riley?" He grabbed his shirt from the floor, where it had been tossed aside the night before, and tugged it on. "Tell me what's wrong."

She swallowed, still unable to form words, and handed him the phone.

He glanced at it and sank back onto his heels. "Oh. Shit."

The shift in his tone cut through her confusion. That wasn't the answer she'd been expecting. Her question was a dry croak. "What?"

"That's horrible." He set the phone on the coffee table, then took her hands in his, concern etched on his face. Something else was there too. She'd gotten far too familiar with it, since he came home. The way he didn't quite meet her gaze. The catch in his voice that meant he was hiding something. "They're morons. They don't know what they're talking about. *Unpolished*, my ass. You're more talented than anyone else ever," he said.

Something wasn't right. "I don't understand how she got my work. I only finished touching up the lines a couple of days ago. I haven't scanned it yet."

His jaw worked up and down for a moment, before any sound came out. "You've got a Deviant Art page. Maybe you've got a reputation."

No. Dread crawled through her. That couldn't be right. She hated herself for thinking it. There was no way he'd betrayed her trust like that. "Literary agents don't go crawling the Internet to have an excuse to reject random people. How did she get my artwork?"

He stood and took a step back, his gaze anywhere but on her. He rubbed the back of his head. "I don't know?"

He was lying to her, but why? "What did you do?"

He hooked his thumbs in the waistband of his shorts, watching his toes trace lines in the carpet. "It wasn't supposed to happen like this. You're skilled and fantastic, and you were getting cold feet, and she was supposed to see how talented you are, and it would be perfect."

"Zane." Please let it be anything but that. A deep, gouging ache of pissed-off started in the center of her chest and spread. "What did you do?"

He finally looked at her again. "I sent her your story, from your email address."

Holy shit, he hadn't. Fury coursed through her, stemming from his nerve—the assumption he had a right—and she clenched her fists until her nails dug into her palms. He'd lied to her about this and gone behind her back, after she told him what she wanted. "That's why you kept my sketchpad for so long."

He shrugged. "I tried to give it back before you missed it."

She rubbed her face, so much happening in her head, she didn't know what to focus on. "You went behind my back." She stood. "I told you I was working on it. I laid out exactly how I felt." She took a step toward him. "After everything we talked about, what made you think you had the right?"

"You deserve this. You weren't taking any steps, and you're better than that. This is motivation. I did it because you deserve better. You need to believe in yourself."

"But that's not up to you." No matter what he said, it couldn't make this better. "All this does is humiliate me. It shows the world how completely and totally untalented I am."

"You're none of that."

"I'm all of that." She was toe to toe with him now, anger flooding her. "You told me *no more secrets*. You said you were done going behind my back. I thought we covered this last night. It's not up to you to decide what is and isn't good for me."

"You covered this last night." A mask slid onto his face, carving his features in stone. "I didn't agree. Not before, not now. If you can't make up your mind, you're going to miss out."

"And that's on me." Frustration lodged in her throat. "Besides, I have made up my mind. I know *exactly* what I want."

"Really? Enlighten me."

"You."

His impassive expression faltered for the briefest second before hardening again. "That's not an option."

His rejection dug deep inside, and left an empty pit. But she promised herself and him this was the last time she'd do this. She made herself clear, and he wasn't interested. Except she couldn't find it in herself to walk away graciously.

"Fuck you." The brush off was easier than giving into the tears stinging her eyelids. She stormed from the apartment and slammed the door behind her, rattling the windows. It took everything she had to make it to her car before the sobs threatening to escape racked her body. Her chest ached, and her throat was raw from biting back the sobs.

Was she more upset with him, for pretending this didn't hurt him as much as her, or with herself, for reading into things that weren't there? Fuck. And why did she want to go back inside and make things better again?

No. They both made their decision. She'd be there for *them* for as long as he wanted, but if he didn't, she couldn't help that.

It took all her focus to make it home, get inside, and lock the world on the other side of the door.

A cry tore from her throat the moment she made it to her bedroom. Tears spilled down her face, and she clutched her sides, trying to keep the shuddering from getting out of control. It wasn't supposed to hurt like this. It wasn't supposed to hurt at all. That was the point of promising *no strings*. It was the reason any of the teasing was okay. It had never been simply teasing, though. It always meant more, despite what they called it.

It hadn't felt like this with Archer or anyone else. The pain of all the guys she'd ever broken up with, put together, didn't ache as much as this. Sinking into depression was the exact opposite of what she wanted.

She dropped down onto her mattress, pulled her knees to her chest, and cried until most of the hurt washed down her cheeks. Her frantic gasps slowed, and she forced herself to take a few deep breaths. Calm crept through her, slowly evicting the desperation.

Life wouldn't end because she couldn't slide her nails up his back and hold him close any more. Forgetting what his lips felt like when they brushed her neck, the hint of five o'clock shadow scuffing her skin, was no big deal.

Watching from a distance while Zane's demons devoured him was far better than doing it up close and personal.

Right?

chapter nineteen

Zane stared at the empty room, trying to smother his thoughts with the same all-encompassing absence of anything. Focusing on the numbness was easier than acknowledging how much every inch of him ached.

Riley was gone. If she was smart, she wasn't coming back. Acid surged in his throat and left a foul taste in his mouth.

When he'd woken up and seen her near tears, then realized why, it slammed into him. He'd done that. He made the same mistake as last time. Let what he wanted—his own selfish wants—hurt someone else.

It was true this was nothing compared to the pain he caused last time. On the other hand, this was Riley. The one person he specifically swore he'd never hurt.

And saying the things he did to her, the way he forced her hand and made her leave, that hurt as much as any of it. He knew what he'd done. Said things meant to push her away. It was better this way in the long run, but it still sucked.

Sabrina was right. Any excuses he came up

with for why he couldn't take the job, all the bullshit about morals, were him lying to himself. He grabbed his phone and dialed Sabrina.

Each ring was another hammer blow against his eardrums. Loud, brash, and shattering. He didn't know if he was relieved or disappointed when her voice mail clicked on. "It's Zane Petrov. Call me back."

He disconnected and let the phone fall to the mattress as he fell back. *Fuck.* The impulse to track down Riley and apologize raced through him. To take it all back and make her smile again. That would make them both feel better now, but it wasn't the best solution long term. She'd recover from this and be happier for it.

He couldn't lie in bed all day, letting his thoughts chase themselves until he was so dizzy he wanted to scream. He needed to get out of here.

Fifteen minutes later, showered, dressed, and no closer to finding his center, he pulled his truck onto the main road and pointed it in a random direction. He wasn't sure where he was going, except south. There wasn't a lot of choice, leaving The Aves.

He followed the roads wherever they went. This time of the morning, there wasn't a lot of traffic to contend with, so it was easy to pick and choose random routes. When he turned down a familiar street, nostalgia and regret hit him hard. How had he not realized he was so close to home?

His old neighborhood looked the same as it had six years ago. And ten. And fifteen, and twenty. Sure, some of the cars and faces were new, but the feeling was still the same.

Riley and Kenzie's mother still lived in their childhood home. Archer and Jen's parents owned the place next door. Granddad's house was around the corner.

Zane parked in front of the brick-faced home he grew up in. He made his way up the driveway but bypassed the front door. This time of day, Granddad would be on the back porch, enjoying the still of the morning. Zane wouldn't have been certain, but he heard the familiar rustle of a newspaper.

He'd stopped by a few times since he got back, but he never stayed long. He wasn't sure why, but something held him back. Now this felt like exactly where he needed to be.

The back yard wasn't big. None of them in the neighborhood were. There was enough space for a clothesline and a deck with a fire pit. Zane and Granddad had built the deck years ago. It only sat six inches off the ground, and despite the worn wood, the stain was fresh and the area clean.

Granddad didn't look up as Zane rounded the corner, but he did fold his newspaper and set it aside. He nodded behind him at the house. "There's fresh coffee inside, and you know where the mugs are." He spoke perfect English—it had been part of his KGB training—but hints of his Russian accent had slipped back in, growing stronger over the years.

"I'm all right. Thank you." Zane settled into the empty wicker chair a few feet away. He glanced sideways at Granddad. After years of denying it, he was about to follow in Granddad's footsteps, as predicted. At least maybe he'd age as well, too.

Granddad's hair had grayed, but it was all still there, and while the man had developed a bit of a gut, it was evident from the way he held himself he was still fit and strong.

Silence settled between them. Zane didn't know what to say or even why he was here, but he didn't feel pressure to fill the empty air.

"Where's your friend?" Granddad's quiet words shattered Zane's attempt at banishing Riley from his thoughts.

"Gone."

"That explains why you look as if she just died. How'd it happen?"

"What?" It took a few seconds for the statement to sink in. "She's not dead. She's probably helping Kenzie with last-minute wedding preparation."

Granddad sank back in his chair. "When did you become so melodramatic? *Gone*. Pft."

Zane almost smiled at the familiar jibe wrapped in sympathy. "Sorry about that."

"How's the cushy life treating you?"

A week ago, he would have said *great*. Aside from the job search, it was exactly what Zane thought he wanted. Then again, a week ago, he'd been lying to himself. "I'm having trouble adjusting." He didn't want to go into details; it had been hard enough recounting it to Riley. Besides, he knew it wasn't expected, and that even though Granddad never talked about it, he'd done worse as KGB. Maybe that was why Zane was here—to find a basis of comparison. That answer felt too easy, though. Despite his granddad's past, Zane had nothing but respect for the man. He wasn't here to compare sins, to make his feel less severe.

"You'll get there." Granddad took a long drink of coffee.

"I'm wondering if I want to."

"Give it time."

"No. You were right about me. I'm not a good person. Time doesn't change that." Was he seeking some form of absolution? Validation? Zane still didn't know. "I have an offer with the CIA…"

"I never should have raised you to be a fucking patriot." For the first time that morning, more than hints of emotion filled the man's words. It sounded like disgust mixed with pity. "I thought it would help you fit in, not be stupid."

Zane was glad he hadn't gotten any coffee, because he'd have choked on it. "Excuse me?"

Granddad finally faced him, the lines on his face looking more distinct and drawn than normal. "I never should have told you the things I did the day you left. I was an old man, sending his boy off to fight for a country I wasn't sure I believed in." It wasn't disgust in his tone, Zane realized. It was regret. "I didn't want to see it break you, so I told myself and you what I needed to hear, to convince me you couldn't be broken."

Zane's mind spun with questions.

"I shouldn't have done it, but I did." Granddad turned his gaze toward the morning sky, and his voice trailed off, as if he were speaking to himself. "You're not a bad kid. In fact, I couldn't be more proud of you."

"I don't…" Zane couldn't find a response. He was used to grudging recognition, but not this raw, bold pride.

"Did your mother ever tell you about your father?" Granddad asked.

The rapid change in subject might have been a relief and given Zane time to figure out how he felt about the confession, but he didn't care for the new topic either. "Nothing more than that he left us." Mom rarely even mentioned the man's name, and Granddad always clammed up when the topic came up, so Zane learned early on not to ask.

"Your *father* was a random asshole your mother hooked up with one summer. Kids are kids, he got her pregnant, and they decided to stay together. I told her she could raise you without him, she insisted they were in love. I didn't like him, and she tried to convince me it was because he'd taken my baby girl from me."

Zane would have smiled at the bit of his past he'd never had a glimpse into before, but there was too much pain in the words.

"I stopped by their apartment one night, to visit, and she was working. You were in your crib, screaming like no baby should be able to, and that asshole was nowhere to be found. He'd left his six-month-old son alone and gone... I didn't know where."

A combination of disgust and indignation swept through Zane, souring in his chest and temporarily giving his frustration something new to focus on. "Then what?"

"I changed you, I poured myself a drink, and I sat down to wait. He stumbled in about two hours later, higher than a fucking kite and reeking of vodka.

Said you were sleeping, so he just stepped out for a quick drink."

Zane wanted to ask *what next*, but he didn't want to interrupt.

Granddad didn't need the prompting. "I told him he had two choices. He could leave right then. Walk out the door and never come back. Never try to find you. Never reach out to your mother again. Vanish completely from your lives. I even handed him the cash he needed, to leave town."

"What was choice number two?"

"He asked me the same thing." Granddad's chuckle held no joy. "I told him he'd vanish either way. He could leave on his own, or no one would see him again, not just the two of you. I wasn't being facetious. I had the power to make it happen. We did a lot of making people disappear back then, and when it came down to that moment, I didn't hesitate. There wasn't a question in my mind I'd do that to him."

Zane knew the things Granddad did in Russia were questionable. Not just from history, but from the distant, haunted look the old man got in his eyes when the subject came up. Still, Zane hadn't expected this. The honesty and reality of it left him feeling raw. Exposed. And at the same time grateful. "I'm glad you made him go."

"I'm not." Granddad shook his head. "I was too, but I've doubted myself so many times since. Don't misunderstand, I was glad he was gone. I regret I didn't let your mother make the decision herself. It was my job to protect you both, but I never should have taken that choice from her. I wouldn't have risked you, but she was smart; she would have made the right call. Especially once I told her what I found when I stopped by your home that day. I needed to trust her, and I didn't."

The story spun in Zane's head, insisting he pay attention. Snarling at him to do more than just stash it as a story about his past. He pushed it aside, unwilling to consider it meant more. "I think you were right. I came out okay because of it."

"I'm pretty lucky there. As long as you're not taking this CIA job for the wrong reasons. Anyway, he would have been gone from your lives regardless, soon enough. Even then, those of us who left the country on a regular basis saw the motherland crumbling, the union falling apart as the Americans bought their way to the forefront of the cold war. I looked at the world around me, the things I'd done, the things about to happen, and I took all of us and bought us into this country."

Zane suspected that much, though he was vague on the details. He knew he wasn't born in the US and it came up when he enlisted, but beyond a mention here and there, it had never caused him any issues.

Granddad sighed. "I didn't leave my past behind, though. I conducted terrible acts under banner of *country*. But I did two things right. I made sure your mother and you made it as far as you did. That doesn't erase my sins, but it helps me atone for them."

Zane knew that feeling more intensely than he wanted to. Except he hadn't done it in the name of patriotism, he'd done it because it was fun. A challenge. "I don't think my reasons were as noble as yours."

"Would you do it again?"

"No." The answer hit Zane hard. Despite the phone call he placed that morning, he couldn't, and he wouldn't.

"Then it's behind you, and now you live right. You let Riley help. I won't lay a guilt trip on you about not throwing away what I gave you. It's your life. But I will be angry if you take it for granted."

It wasn't that simple. Zane didn't have any illusions about flipping a switch and being okay with what had happened. But he couldn't find the words to argue. "Yes, Sir."

They chatted for a while longer, about random banal things. The weather. Sports. Politics. But Zane couldn't focus on the conversation. Too many thoughts warred for his attention. When he left, he felt like he had more answers and more questions than ever before.

He did know one thing, though. He sent Sabrina a quick text as he walked back to his truck.

My final answer's no. Don't ask again. At least that was one right decision.

chapter twenty

"Mother." Riley smiled and gave her a polite hug. Nothing too tight that might wrinkle the satin of her mother's dress or stress her skin.

Riley relied on every ounce of willpower she had to maintain her composure for Kenzie's wedding. It had been almost a week since she'd talked to Zane, and despite her resolution to leave him be, not seeing him made her miserable. However, she'd do almost anything for her sister, including smile and nod at each of Mother's passive-aggressive comments.

Her mother's hair—blonde, like her daughters'—was piled on top of her head. She held Riley at arm's length, gaze raking over her appraisingly. "You look good, hon. Kenzie picked a nice dress for you."

Riley clenched her jaw. She gave her mother a tight smile. "Thank you."

Mother—Riley and Kenzie weren't allowed to call her *Mom* or *Sharon* or anything else, always *Mother*—smoothed something on the side of Riley's head. "You really could have done a better job with your hair."

Embarrassment flooded Riley, and she hated the flush rising to her skin. "Sorry."

"No one will be watching you anyway." Mother waved a hand and turned back to the bride.

Riley sank against a nearby wall, arms crossed over her chest.

"Don't slouch, hon." Her mother never looked up as she moved the flowers woven through Kenzie's hair a fraction of an inch. "Do I get to meet your date?"

Riley's gaze met Kenzie's in the mirror, and Kenzie gave her an apologetic half-smile. Riley loved her mother dearly, but at times like this, she remembered exactly why she'd gone to live with her father after her parents' divorce, when she and Kenzie were in their late teens.

"Riley's a strong, independent woman," Kenzie said. "She doesn't need a date to attend a wedding."

Mother's sniff said she felt otherwise. She turned her attention back to Riley. "Maybe your sister can hook you up with one of the groom's guests. He seems like he knows a number of respectable people."

Riley bit back her snort, trying to keep her dry amusement off her face. She knew she didn't completely succeed. "Maybe." The majority of Scott's friends made Riley's look positively uptight by comparison.

Shaking her head, Mother peeked outside at the guests streaming into the wedding hall. "At least you didn't bring one of those boys who treats you like one of them."

Riley's gut clenched at the reminder of Zane

and Archer. Mostly of Zane.

"Mother, will you grab my shoes?" Kenzie asked.

"Of course, dear." Mother looked at Riley again. "There's a handsome young man out there who looks like he might be military. Maybe your sister can introduce you to him."

"I think they've met." Kenzie stood and slipped into her heels, growing by four inches.

Riley swallowed back the sick feeling. If the reminder of Zane didn't hurt so much, she might tell Mother that's who she was talking about. She'd seen him come in, and that he looked incredible in his tux was one thing she agreed with her mother about.

A knock interrupted the interrogation. "Are you ladies decent?"

Riley yanked open the door enough to let her father in.

He threw his arms around her, lifted her in a bear hug, and squeezed her. "Hey, baby."

"Daddy." At least there was some comfort there.

He started toward Kenzie, pausing when Mother glared at him. Instead of hugging her tight, he settled for a kiss on the cheek. "You both look lovely."

The organ music started. Mother extracted herself from the group, shooting one last glare at Riley and her father. "Make sure my baby girl makes it to the altar okay."

"It's a room away, Sharon. They'll both survive."

Mother didn't look as though she believed him

but left to lead the wedding procession.

Riley grabbed her sister's hands, looking back at that mirror image. She forced her own grief aside and gave Kenzie a genuine smile. "I'm really happy for you."

Kenzie grinned back. "Thanks."

Riley squeezed one last time, before letting go, to take her place in line where she'd fall into step next to the best man. "See you on the other side."

Zane found a wall away from everyone and leaned against it. He tilted his head back, studying the ceiling. When he closed his eyes, the afterimage of lights danced with women in taffeta and men dressed like penguins. He sighed and straightened.

Focusing on the reception again, he let his gaze trip across faces. So many were familiar. He was glad most of them already said their awkward *welcome backs*, told him he looked good, and moved on. Kenzie and Scott stood at the far end of the room, shaking hands and accepting congratulations. Zane had been near them long enough to know some were sincere and some were obligatory, and that Kenzie kept a quiet but tight leash on them, making sure they all came off sounding the same.

He knew there were unwritten rules about the bridesmaid not looking as good as the bride, but if it hadn't been for the subtle but constant cloud of depression hanging over Riley, she would have stolen the night, even though the two women were technically identical. Then again, maybe he was biased.

Ignoring Riley was destroying him, but he was determined not to break.

Someone stopped behind her. Archer stood close, hand resting on her arm. She bent her head to his and responded to something he said.

Zane knocked back the rest of his punch. Time to check out the bar. He pushed away from the wall, looking anywhere but at the wedding line.

He ordered bourbon, neat, and shuffled back into the crowd. At least at a party this big, it wasn't too hard to lose himself, except the crowds thinned as the night wore on. Why was he sticking around? Probably because he hadn't convinced himself not to talk to Riley. Failed to ignore the desire to see if she wanted to hang out… Or more. He glanced back toward where the wedding party had been, but they'd dispersed.

He almost turned away again, before he caught a glimpse of movement in the dark, several feet back. Unmistakably Riley and Archer, standing near each other, away from anyone else. Talking.

It was time for him to take off. He spun to leave.

"Watch out." A pair of hands clasped his shoulders, jarring him to a stop.

Fuck. He wasn't in the mood for this.

"You know"—Scott nodded at Zane's untouched drink—"if you don't want that…"

Zane shoved the bourbon in his direction. "Help yourself."

"Not for me." Scott tugged Kenzie closer, his arm wrapped around her waist. "I need something to ply the bride with, for our honeymoon."

Disgust crawled through Zane. This guy was

worse than he thought.

Kenzie rolled her eyes, took the drink from him, and set it on a nearby table. "He's yanking your chain. Give me some credit."

"I knew that," Zane mumbled. "Again, you look beautiful." He squeezed Kenzie's fingertips. "Congratulations one last time, before I bolt for the night."

"Thanks, and we're doing the same real soon." Kenzie pretty much glowed.

"Handsome, upstanding military man like you, leaving alone?" Scott elbowed him.

The dig hit exactly the wrong nerve. "Yes." Zane's tone was flat.

"Didn't mean to imply anything." Scott held up his hands. "I've got a programmer who's been eying you all night. If he's more your type…"

Zane stared at him, irritation kicking into overdrive. "I'm fine, thanks."

"He knows exactly who you've got your eye on," Kenzie interjected. "He's trying to poke holes in who you are and find your weak spots."

"I'm… being trolled? Are you six?" Zane shifted his weight and crossed his arms. Though he couldn't beat the other man when it came to muscle bulk, he had at least a couple inches on him and wanted to make it clear he wasn't backing down.

Scott smirked. "Only on my best days."

"You have five minutes." Kenzie kissed Scott on the cheek and melted back into the crowds.

"Yes, Ma'am." Scott paced a few feet, his gaze following the crowds, before he turned back to face Zane. "You must be something pretty special."

Zane's gut sank when he realized he was facing Riley again. She wasn't tucked into the dark corner anymore, but she was still talking to Archer. Her arms were crossed, but they stood close. He needed to leave.

He forced his attention back to Scott. "I have a feeling this line of conversation is a barrel of chuckles for you, but it's getting old for me." Part of Zane knew he was being rude. Most of him didn't know if it mattered or even if he cared.

"You never called." Scott rested a hand on his arm.

Zane stepped away, brows raised. "You were expecting me to? It was just dinner."

Scott laughed. "Nice. Very clever. I'll try this a different way, since the business card didn't clue you in. I know who you are."

"I'm a friend of your wife's." He hated that was all he felt comfortable saying. For so long he'd almost felt like family, and now he was relegated to *bride's guest* and nothing more.

"Keep telling yourself that's all, but it won't make it any truer." Scott loosened his tie. "But I was talking about The Taurus."

Jesus. Zane wasn't as willing to own the pseudonym as he had been with Mikki. She'd been in awe. Who the fuck knew what Scott was thinking? "That's supposed to mean something to me?"

"You're not what I expected." Scott rocked on the balls of his feet, occasionally obstructing the view of Riley and Archer. "I mean, the abrasive attitude and arrogance makes sense, but I thought I'd get a lot more ego and bragging from the guy who used to practically paint forums with his name and antics."

Had Riley really talked about him that much? The thought would have warmed him if he couldn't see her in the background, relaxing. "That was a persona. Besides, I've grown up."

"I hope not too much." Scott snapped his fingers. "Am I boring you?"

Zane tried to keep an eye on Riley and participate in the conversation at the same time. "I'm fine. Didn't you have a time limit?"

"Right. Seven years ago, you hacked our security and released a moderately intensive demo of our game to the public six weeks early."

Oh yeah. That had been one of his favorites. *Shit*. Scott's company name had been different back then, but Zane should have known it was familiar. "That was you? Um… oops?" That wasn't really the most sincere apology he could have come up with. Did he care? Not unless Scott was going to press charges, and for as much as the guy seemed like an ass, Zane didn't think that was too likely. "I was a kid. I didn't know any better."

"You were in your early twenties. Old enough to drink and vote. Not quite a kid." Scott's expression was laced with a smile still, no irritation present. "I don't want an *I'm sorry*. It was some of the best publicity we ever had. It put us on the map."

"You're welcome?"

Scott shrugged and looked over his shoulder, following Zane's continuously drifting line of sight. "She looks good, doesn't she?"

Zane shook his head and tore his gaze away

from Riley. Mostly. "I suppose."

"Even if you hadn't spent the entire time I was here staring at her, I wouldn't be arrogant enough to think I looked better than she does." Scott glanced at his watch. "I have less than a minute, so I'll make this fast. It was good publicity then. The Internet works differently now, and something like that could topple us. I need someone on board who can keep someone like you from doing it again. The job is yours if you want it."

Zane was now ninety-nine percent focused on the conversation. "Wait. What?"

"You heard me."

That had been one of the biggest hacks he'd ever done, not because of the attention it garnered, but because it had been a challenge. Regardless of how conceited this jackass was, Zane was being offered a chance to do it again, but better, and for money. One thing held him back. "I don't take pity jobs."

Scott's laugh drew a couple of stares from people nearby. "Pity? I must not have groveled enough. Or did you miss the genuine awe? I'm a hundred-percent serious."

Zane stalled on his response, not sure what to say. The offer sounded real, but part of him couldn't accept it. "Why would I work for you?"

"Probably not for the money, though I promise the paycheck is worth it, and you won't mind the signing bonus. Maybe because you know it will be a challenge. Or, if that's not enough, because it gives you a chance to put me in my place, by poking holes in my security."

Take it, take it, take it. His stubborn streak won out. "Still not convinced."

"I'll be back in two weeks. You have until then to decide."

"Right. I'll be in touch," Zane replied, faster than he meant to. He wanted this. He wasn't going to bluff himself out of a once-in-a-lifetime opportunity. "You already know I'm going to say *yes*, don't you?"

Scott's grin widened. "Let's just say I hoped. Two weeks, we'll negotiate. Make sure you can at least buy my baby sister the ring she deserves."

Zane's temper rose again. "Not your decision, probably not my job, and realistically doesn't look like it's happening any time soon."

"Right. Keep lying to yourself."

"Why are you so focused on my relationship with Riley?" Zane raised his voice and winced, drawing his emotions back under a tight leash when a few more nearby heads turned. Fortunately, the party had thinned considerably, and the band was still loud enough that not a lot of people heard.

"She means the world to Kenzie. So in turn, she means the world to me."

Zane gritted his teeth. "You don't have any idea what that means."

"Really? You're going to tell me on my own wedding day that I don't know what love is? I'm not getting into that pissing match." Scott extended his hand. "I won't mention her again. Call me in two weeks."

Zane reluctantly shook his hand and nodded over Scott's shoulder. "Thing is, it doesn't matter how I feel if she doesn't feel the same."

Riley was pushing out a side door with Archer, the two standing close, heads bowed together.

Scott's smirk faded for the first time that night. "I'm sorry."

"Me too. Enjoy Cancun."

chapter twenty-one

Zane lay in bed, staring at the ceiling as the morning light crested the mountains. It was still dark outside, but the first glow of early morning creeped across the valley. He rubbed his dry eyes and blinked, trying to find some moisture somewhere. He rolled his head to the side, and the red numbers on his clock glared back at him. Almost seven. Apparently he wasn't going to sleep any time soon.

He kicked out of bed and pulled on whatever was nearby. A pale-gray business card winked back at him from its isolated spot on the edge of the coffee table. At least something good had come out of the night before, even though he couldn't find an ounce of enthusiasm for it.

He still didn't know what to do about Riley. The sleepless night, combined with watching her buddy up to Archer, had destroyed his resolve to keep her at arm's length. Granddad's voice whispered in the back of his mind, asking if he was taking Riley's decision from her again, like he had with her sketches. If remaining silent about the fact that he loved her was wrong.

He grabbed his wallet and keys and headed out

to his truck. He needed to make sense of the jumble of information bouncing in his skull. One thought rang true, though. He couldn't ignore her any longer. He wanted her in his life, as more than a friend. She might no longer feel the same, after his childish efforts to scare her away, but it had to be her choice.

He typed out a brief text message.

I'm sorry. Give me a chance to apologize in person.

His gut sank when he looked up and realized Archer's car wasn't on the street. Or in the parking lot. Or anywhere in sight. Had he really not come home the night before?

Zane bit back his doubt and hit *Send*. He climbed in his truck and pulled into traffic. Habit almost made him turn toward the coffee shop where he and Riley always met, but he didn't think he could face it that morning. He wasn't sure which put him more on edge—that she might be there or that he might never see her there again. Instead of having to face either, he turned in the other direction, toward the other side of town.

Twenty minutes later, he found a seat in the back of a coffee shop filled with eclectic décor. The place had been designed to look random and hip, but every single piece of art, catchy phrase, and polka dot on the walls and furniture was strategically placed. He cringed at the cold feeling of the place, watching people come and go. No one stuck around for longer than it took to get their drinks. This wasn't the kind of place where people hung out. They were only there for the label on the cup.

He sighed and sank back into the stiff vinyl

bench. In a couple of weeks, he'd be able to stomach the other spot again, but for now, he'd have to remember how to work the coffeemaker at home.

He pulled Scott's business card from his back pocket and turned it over in his fingers, trying to find the enthusiasm to be happy about the entire thing. Chance of a lifetime, and Zane couldn't even muster a fake *woo-hoo*.

He looked up when the front door chimed, and he had to do a double take.

Riley paused a few feet away, eyes wide and gaze locked on him.

His pulse skidded and stuttered, and his heart hammered. He forced himself to smile. To pretend she hadn't ignored his text. To overlook that she still wore her bridesmaid dress. That her hair had torn itself from the high bun she'd had it in, six hours before, and it fell in messy locks around her shoulders. That her makeup was smeared, her cheeks were flushed, and her lips swollen.

"Hey." Her voice was so soft it vanished in the hip background music. "What's that?" She nodded at his hand.

Not how he intended to start this conversation, but he'd take any opener. He held the business card up between his index and middle finger. "Your brother-in-law's business card. He offered me a job."

The corner of her mouth twitched, but he couldn't tell if it wanted to pull up or down. "Congratulations." Her voice was flat.

He tried to keep his tone light. "If this is what nepotism gets me, what happens when he finds out how severely I fucked up?" He winced as the words passed his lips. He hadn't meant to sound so bitter.

Her shoulders slumped. "He doesn't work like that. If he offered you the job, it has nothing to do with me. It's because he wants you working for him."

He reached deep inside and pulled out a smile. "I'm sorry—"

She cut him off. "I got your message. Couldn't answer. I'll just tell you in person. We lost that chance."

He furrowed his brow and studied her face, looking for some sign of forgiveness or hatred—or anything. All he saw was his confusion reflected back at him. "Then…"

She shook her head. "I have to get home."

"Wait." This conversation couldn't end like this. He finally understood what Granddad's point was. What it meant. How it applied to him. Even if Riley didn't forgive him, he owed her an apology. "About what I said…"

She locked a sad gaze on him but didn't interrupt.

"I shouldn't have done or said any of it. Except tell you the truth about what happened while I was gone. You deserve to know, or our friendship isn't as strong as I want to think it is. I've been unfair to you for too long." Now that the words tumbled out, he needed to keep going. "I'm used to people having a hidden agenda, to them not saying what they mean—and that's my problem, not yours—but I know you don't work that way. I know I can trust you.

"I'm so sorry I betrayed you, and I don't expect you to say it's all cool and just forget about it. And I know some of it you might not ever be able to overlook. And I love you, Riley. I always have, and it's okay if you don't feel the same, but you deserve to know."

She ran her thumb over each of her fingernails, not quite looking at him. Her expression wavered, and she chewed on the inside of her cheek. "Thank you."

Not even close to what he expected. "Of course."

She hesitated for a moment, before kissing him on the cheek—quick and chaste, the way she had so many times over the years. Then she turned and walked out, never making it to the counter for her own drink.

His entire frame tensed at the lack of resolution, until his head throbbed and his neck ached. Had he been forgiven? Did it matter? Were she and Archer back together? Again? For the five billionth time?

They must have spent the night together. Why else would she still be dressed like that? That would explain why she had such a neutral response to his gut-wrenching revelation. He'd known she might not feel the same, but her brush-off dug deep, aching in his chest and throbbing in his skull.

He tossed his mostly full cup in the trash and walked out the door. On top of everything else, he needed to figure out if he really could be happy for Riley, regardless of who she ended up with.

He sank in his truck and leaned back into the headrest. He didn't know if he was capable of working that hard, to atone for his sins.

♥ ♥ ♥

Riley forced her eyes open and blinked several times to loosen the mascara caked with dried tears holding her lids shut. Falling asleep in her wedding makeup had been a bad idea. Falling asleep crying had been a bad idea. She should have said something different to Zane this morning. The last twenty-four hours of her life seemed a clusterfuck of things she should have done differently.

She shook her head and sat up.

He loved her. Three words that never meant anything until they came from him. A confession that drilled into her heart and filled her soul… And she'd frozen and brushed him off, stalled on her own insecurities.

The sun was sinking behind the mountains outside. Had she really slept through the day? Before her head had hit the pillow, she'd thought she might never be able to sleep again.

She climbed from her bed and shuffled into the shower, dropping clothes as she went. The spray of icy water hit her face, waking her up. She closed her eyes and leaned into the stream, letting it wash away too many layers of everything as it warmed up.

The longer she thought about it, and after the time she'd spent with Archer over the last few days, she knew she couldn't be angry with Zane. It hurt too much to hold the grudge, and even worse, to not have him in her life. What he did was so very wrong. Not while he was deployed—though she still struggled with those decisions, and it would take time for both of them to deal with. But what he'd said about her not knowing herself, and his going behind her back… She needed to believe he meant it when he said he would never do it again. At the same time, it lit a fire under her butt and forced her to admit things she might not have otherwise.

She scrubbed off everything she could, until her skin was pink and raw, and then shut off the water and dried herself. She didn't drag her feet quite so much on the carpet. The more she woke up, the more glimpses of the night before—or had it been early morning?—drifted back to her. The things she'd decided, the resolutions she'd made, the promises that had stuck in her head and evaporated in exhaustion and surprise when she talked to Zane.

She grabbed some of the most comfortable clothes she could find, including a T-shirt she'd stolen from Zane in high school and never given back, got dressed, and then sat down to work.

She didn't know if she had the courage to do what she was about to, but if she didn't, it would ache inside forever. Knowing she had to take this next step was the big reason she wasn't still mad at Zane. Sure, he'd gone behind her back, and he'd lied to her. That would have to change, but he'd never done it before, so she believed him when he said he was sorry.

Besides, it had given her the strength to make this decision and had finally pushed her in the right direction. She opened her sketchbook, booted up her computer and large-format scanner, and began taking high-resolution digital shots of the graphic novel she'd spent the last few years over-polishing.

As the computer hummed and the scanner whirred, her attention fell on her phone. It still sat on her desk, taunting her. Zane's message was on there.

She breathed deep and dialed his number.

"Riley?" Hope and hesitation poured from his greeting.

She smiled with relief. "Hey. What are you up to?"

"You know." His casual tone sounded forced. "Nothing, really. I'm not in the mood to game, and there's nothing good on TV, and—"

"Come over?" She cut him off before his ramble could get awkward. "I mean... that is... do you want to hang out?"

"God, yes."

Her smile grew. "We need to talk. I mean it may not be all fun and games. It may get serious for a little bit." Why was she over-explaining herself in the vaguest terms possible?

"I don't care. Don't take that wrong, I care what you have to say, and whatever it is, I'm listening. What's up?"

She couldn't do this over the phone. She needed to see his face, to get it right. "Come over, and I'll tell you."

"Hmm... a bribe. Or blackmail. I'll be there soon."

She let out a small laugh as she disconnected and set the phone aside. The gnawing uncertainty was still there, lingering in the back of her thoughts, but she already felt better. Now she had to focus on her scanning and keep her thoughts from running too rampant, while she waited for him to show up.

chapter twenty-two

Zane hesitated outside Riley's door, trying to bring down his racing pulse. She'd called him. She sounded happy to talk to him, but she wanted a serious conversation. That was either great news or not. She didn't mention his confession that morning, and he didn't know how to interpret that. He raised his hand to knock, and the door flew open before his knuckles pulled away from the first rap.

Riley's cheeks were pink. He was pretty sure that had been his shirt at one point, but his had been black, and hers was kind of a dark gray, so maybe not. Either way— "You look gorgeous."

"Thanks." She let him in and shut the door behind him, hovering a few feet back. "That was fast."

He shrugged. *Not fast enough.* He'd never noticed how many lights and signs were between her place and his before.

"You look good too." She stepped around him, keeping her distance, and nodded toward her bedroom. "I need to show you something."

His imagination tried to kick in, taunting him with every definition imaginable of what that meant.

He told it to go to hell and shoved the images back down. There was something off in the way she walked, an awkward hesitation combined with the occasional glance over her shoulder, as he followed her.

She dropped into her computer chair. The mouse cursor on the screen wavered, betraying the slight shake to her hand. "So, um…"

He waited for her to finish her thought, attention on her profile. The uncertain way she caught her lip between her teeth, the flicker of her eyes between the screen and not quite at him, was alluring and disquieting at the same time. "What's up?" he finally prompted.

She took a deep breath and spun in her chair, facing her computer. "I decided you were right."

Fantastic. "About what?"

"I need to stop hesitating and just get my artwork out there. It's true that no one may want it, but I'll never know unless I try, right?"

"Right." He wanted to grin that she was taking this step, and felt selfish for being disappointed instead. Not by the news—he screamed for joy inside about that—but he'd been hoping to hear something else. Something more about the two of them.

She let out a small laugh, the most incredible sound he'd heard in days. "You probably already know this—I hope you already know this—but I have to send samples of my work along with my query, and I need to pick my best pages. Since you spoofed my email, I don't know which images you picked." She turned her full attention on him for the first time since he'd arrived. "I have my favorites, but

I can't decide. I'm hoping some of them are your favorites too, so I can narrow my choices down. Help me pick some out?"

"Of course." A tinge of relief floated through him. It wasn't a confession of love, but it was the friendship he had been terrified they'd lost. He could work with that. He'd take that over nothing in a heartbeat.

She nodded her head toward the monitor. "You can get closer if you want. You know, so you can see. I promise it's okay."

He closed the distance between them. As she flipped through the scans, he couldn't hide his awe at her talent. It made it hard to choose, but they slowly narrowed down the selection. Excitement danced on her face the more they got into it.

He settled his hand on the back of her chair, leaning in to get a closer look at the details. He saw now why it had been a mistake to send off her unfinished work, aside from the severe breach-of-trust issue. What he'd been impressed with before was nothing compared to the studio quality he looked at now.

She leaned back, resting against him as they dove into the final selection process. She was still torn deciding between two panels. He traced light lines along her shoulder blade, relieved when she didn't pull away.

"How's Archer?" The question slipped out before he could stop it, and he cringed.

Her back went stiff, and she sat straight up. "Fine, I suppose."

"Happy to have you back?" God damn it, he

was being a jerk.

She dropped her head and sighed.

He'd ruined the moment. He might as well get it over with. Find out what was really going on, wish her luck—because that's what friends did—and all that bullshit. "You two make a cute couple."

She winced, and a small squeak tore from her throat. Something that was half-whimper, half-sigh. "What happened to *he's a clingy jackass*?"

Zane shrugged. "Whatever works for him."

She tilted her head back for a moment, eyes closed. Then she stood and faced him, gaze locked on his. "You really think we make a cute couple?"

Yes. He needed to say *yes*. He had to do this. He had to be supportive. "No. I still think he's a clingy jackass and you deserve so much better. You already said you didn't love him."

Her pained expression melted away. "How do you really feel?"

"Clever. I already bore my heart, and you didn't take it quite the way I hoped."

Her threatening smile wavered. "Nothing happened with Archer," she said softly. "I mean, not *nothing*, but I didn't sleep with him. Or anything else that involved him touching me in any way."

Zane swallowed, not daring to hope. His heartbeat echoed in his ears. "You were still wearing your bridesmaid dress this morning."

"Yeah, I was."

"So you never made it home." This was killing him. He clenched his jaw. "It didn't look like he did either."

A soft smile danced under the sadness on her

face. "I don't know where he was. After we left the wedding, we went for coffee. We talked. A lot. I apologized for leading him on then shutting him out. He apologized for being a clingy, presumptuous jackass."

Zane couldn't hide his disbelief, but he refused to give into the hint of amusement. "His words?"

Her smile grew. "My words, his meaning."

"That took all night?"

"I walked away when he started droning on about how I made a mistake leaving him."

"You shouldn't have to put up with that."

"I didn't." She stepped closer. "You have a pretty strong opinion about what I do and don't deserve. Have you ever stopped to think nothing would make me happier than you?"

He stopped breathing for a moment, not sure he'd heard her right.

She kept going. "I said *goodbye* to him after an hour or so, thanked him for everything, and drove around until I was too tired to do so safely. I was trying to convince myself to stay away from you, since you already pushed me out twice. Telling myself you didn't love me the way I do you. You almost broke me in the coffee shop, but I managed to keep it all in until I got home."

His heart leaped in his throat at the words. Jesus, she'd taken her time getting there, but he still loved the way it sounded. "What did you figure out?"

"I didn't." She reached for him then dropped her arm again. "My brain spun in on itself over and over again, until I thought I might pass out on my feet from exhaustion, and when you said it this morning—actually said, *I love you*—I thought I was hallucinating. Tell me you meant it?"

Relief surged through him. He wrapped his fingers in her hair, pulled her close, and kissed her hard, not breaking away until he couldn't breathe. He gasped as they broke apart. He held her head in place, gaze locked on hers. "I love you more than anything. I don't know what I'd do without you. Just thinking about waking up someplace that you'll never be coming back to hurts more than I want to dwell on."

It felt incredible to have the words out. Especially when she shifted her weight, pressing into him. "Me too."

She kissed him again, hungry and desperate, digging her nails into his back. When she pulled away, he realized what he'd missed that morning. Her face looked almost exactly the same, except relief and joy danced in her eyes now instead of red-rimmed grief.

He spun and dropped into her chair, grabbed her hands in his, and tugged her to stand between his legs. "I should have said something sooner. I should have told you so many things sooner."

She bent and silenced him with a quick kiss before stepping away. "It doesn't matter. It's out now. Whatever happened while you were gone doesn't change how I feel about you. I'm not sure my acceptance matters, but I know why you made the decisions you did, and if you had any idea at all what they would lead to, you wouldn't have done it."

She had more faith in him than he did, but that went both ways when it came to them. He didn't forgive himself, but he had a feeling he'd get there.

"It means a lot. Thank you."

"Beyond that, all I care about is that we stop hiding things from each other. Well, I care about other things, too. I mean, I'm pretty hardcore infatuated with you, and this whole artwork thing, and that I didn't get laid after my sister's wedding. Isn't that like a bridesmaid's right or something?"

He couldn't hold back his laughter. "At least you have your priorities, and yes, if we're to believe popular media—and really, why wouldn't we?—you're definitely owed that."

She bit her bottom lip, hands shoved in her front pockets and tugging down the waistband of her jeans. "So are you volunteering?"

He made a show of looking around him. "Are you offering it to anyone else?"

"Nope. Just making sure."

He hesitated. Should he do what he wanted? It hadn't been a problem in the past, but so many significant things had changed.

She fiddled with the bottom of her T-shirt. "Your move."

His pulse whirred into overdrive, and he smirked. The things that mattered were still the same. He needed to remember that. "You're sure?"

She ducked her head, watching him through thick lashes, pink covering her cheeks. "I trust you."

The words slammed home harder than they ever had before, and he realized how much she meant when she said that. Jesus. He'd been an idiot. At least she'd given him another chance. The revelation kicked his arousal up a gear.

He leaned back in the chair, watching her. The

way she was flushed, waiting, and wanting as she shifted her weight from one foot to the other, always studying him.

"Take off your shirt."

Her smile grew. She crossed her arms, grabbed the hem of her T-shirt, and pulled it over her head, pausing with her arms raised, elongating the lines and curves of her slender frame and drawing attention to her bare breasts.

She tossed the top aside and returned her thumbs to her jeans pockets. Her chest heaved with every nervous breath, exposed nipples hardening, and her flat stomach vanished teasingly into low-rise denim. He could almost taste the memories of running his lips over her skin. "Jeans next."

"Yes, Sir." Her fingers were nimble undoing the button, and then she slowly slid down the zipper. She pushed the jeans past her hips, revealing high-cut panties, and let them fall the rest of the way to the floor. Bending at the waist, she stepped out of one leg at a time before tossing the clothing aside.

For as many times as he'd been called *sir* in the past few years, he'd thought it was just a word. Hearing her say it fuzzed his thoughts and heightened his senses. She grabbed her left arm with her right hand and licked her lips. Her gaze flickered toward the closet for the briefest moment before returning to him.

His dick pulsed, straining against his jeans. He crossed the room in a few long strides, only having to study the built-in shelves for a moment before finding what he was looking for.

He grabbed two silk scarves and padded up

behind her. He slid his hands down her arms and pulled her back against him. "I always wondered why you collected these if you never actually wore them."

She leaned into him with a soft sigh. "No one ever figures it out. Another reason to love you."

Love. He did like the way she said that. He bound her wrists loosely behind her with one scarf and glided his lips along the back of her neck. "Did you ever tell anyone else you might be interested?"

A whimper slipped from her throat. "Maybe I was never interested with anyone else."

He pressed against her back, memorizing every inch of her yielding frame against him. He brought the second scarf up, and she let out a tiny gasp when he covered her eyes and tied it behind her head.

He dropped his hands to her hips, inching forward to run his palms up her stomach and cup her breasts.

She leaned back her head, her moan growing louder when he pinched her nipples. He wanted to take her now. His cock strained, begging to drive deep inside her, but even more, he wanted to stretch this moment out. Make sure they both enjoyed it.

He continued to tweak and pull the sensitive nubs. Her hips swayed in rhythm with the motion. She raised her bound hands out of the way enough to grind her ass against him. Her breath came in shorter gasps, the longer he abraded them.

She stood straight when he pulled away. A mewl escaped when he rested his hands on her hips again.

He hooked his thumbs in the elastic of her

panties, brushing the bare skin underneath, and tugged. He slid the underwear down her legs, the scent of her arousal taunting him, and gently lifted each foot so he could toss the clothing aside.

He nudged her toward the chair, guiding her so she didn't trip or run into anything, and helped her sit, arms still bound behind her back.

She licked her lips, her breathing shallow.

chapter twenty-three

Riley kept her eyes closed. There was no point in looking with the scarf in her way. Every other sense was heightened. The fabric of the low-backed chair was warm and rough against her bare skin. She strained her ears for any sound, but her hammering pulse made it difficult to tell what was important.

She was slick with want, growing wetter every second as the anticipation built.

Her hair was swept across her back and pushed over her shoulder, sending a pleasant chill through her. She inhaled sharply at the brush of Zane's lips on her neck.

He nipped her earlobe, sucking lightly before releasing it again. "You're incredible."

The compliment, combined with the husky sound of his voice, sent goose bumps over her. She sighed and leaned into the sensation. "You're pretty amazing too."

His chuckle vibrated against her skin, and then he pulled away again. Cool air caressed her body leaving her wondering and wanting. *What next?*

As the seconds ticked away, her pulse raced faster, and her ears strained harder. She whimpered in anticipation when rough fabric scraped between her legs, forcing them apart. Denim, maybe? His knee? Not that it mattered. Air rushed to greet her damp mound.

When his lips brushed the inside of her leg near her knee, a pulse of need started in her gut and traveled down. He kissed a slow, light trail along her inner thigh, moving up one leg and down the other, never getting close to her aching sex.

She scooted forward on the chair, blindly trying to get closer, and the contact stopped.

"Impatient, much?" His teasing growl echoed through the room.

"A little." She tried to keep her tone light.

"Only a little."

"Okay. A lot." She swallowed, desire flooding her. "I'll beg if it will help."

A heavy pause hung in the air before he finally said, "Not today."

She gasped, butt coming off the chair, when his finger traced her slit. Seconds later, his tongue followed the same path, tearing a moan from her. He licked along the slick skin, drawing closer to her clit with each pass, but never touching it.

When he finally flicked over the swollen nub, she cried out, nearly coming from the single touch. He wrapped his mouth around it, licking and occasionally nibbling in time to the thrust of her hips.

A climax built inside. Every inch of her was alive, feeling everything. There was no warning before he shoved his fingers inside her, opening her wide and filling her up. The new sensation pushed her over the edge, and she clenched around him as she came.

His attentions slowed with her, shifting from hungry sucking to tiny kisses before stopping. He pulled away, leaving her isolated again.

Her head swam, euphoria mingling with the electric anticipation of not being able to see where he was or what he was doing.

"Stand up." His voice was close, but she couldn't tell where it came from.

She obeyed, warmth spreading between her legs again.

His heat brushed her back but he didn't make contact.

He turned and guided her, stopping when her shins nudged the edge of the bed.

"Lie as close to the middle as you can. On your side." His words caressed her ear, his voice low.

He helped guide her as she climbed clumsily onto the bed, the action hindered by her bound hands and blindfolded eyes.

Then there was nothing again. No voice, touch, or sounds.

She lay on her side, breathing shallowly. Was that a rustle of clothes or just her ear against the comforter?

"I want"—his voice near her ear startled her—"to feel all of you. No protection. Are you okay with that?"

She couldn't hide her smile at the request disguised as simple, but meaning so much more. She forced her voice to stay steady. "Yes."

He kissed her cheek, the light touch lingering for a moment before he was gone again.

Time ticked away, feeling exaggerated in the artificial darkness. The mattress shifted with a new weight, and her heart leapt into her throat, expectation screaming through every inch of her.

Zane's hands slid up her leg, hooked under her knee, and brought her foot to rest on the bed, so one leg was propped, the other still reclined like the rest of her. Skin brushed her extended leg. She assumed he was straddling her.

He slid his fingers along her slit, nudging the edge of her opening but not going farther. She gasped in pleasure when the head of his cock followed the same path, but didn't slide inside, and then he pushed in from behind, driving deep into her before pulling almost all the way out again.

He thrust back inside her, hips slapping her butt as his rhythm increased. One hand gripped her knee, the other holding her hip as he plunged into her repeatedly. Her climax built again, rushing in fast, and she gasped as she came, clenching around his shaft and riding the long orgasm as he pounded hard and fast.

His breathing shifted to sharp grunts, and she knew he was close too. His rhythm became more frantic, rising to a heated pace before slowing and stopping.

She lay there, listening to their mingled breathing, focused on him still buried in her. He kissed the top of her knee, lips lingering on her skin, before unwinding himself from her legs.

With a few gentle tugs, the scarf fell away from her wrists. She arched her back, loosening up her shoulders.

"You're okay, right?" His voice was close, heavy with concern and still breathless.

She smiled big. "I'm absolutely fantastic."

He chuckled, and the mattress shifted again. Seconds later, the blindfold fell away. She blinked at the sudden light, glad it wasn't brighter.

He lay next to her, propped up on one elbow, raking his gaze over her face. "You're absolutely amazing."

She flushed and ducked her head. He rested a finger under her chin and pulled her face back up. He kissed her hard, crushing his lips against hers, holding her in place and stealing her breath.

They broke apart, and she shifted on the bed, burying her forehead against his chest. "I'm definitely completely, totally, and madly in love with you."

He trailed his fingers through her hair. "Ditto."

chapter twenty-four

Riley drummed her fingers on the plastic table and resisted the urge to check her phone for the fifty-millionth time in thirty seconds. Where was he? Steam had stopped rising from the coffee cups in front of her—one untouched and one mostly drained—at least half an hour ago.

It had been two weeks since they told each other *I love you,* and the rush of knowing he felt the same still hadn't worn off. She didn't know that it ever would. He'd all but moved in since. He grumbled this morning about having to go to work for the first time in forever, but she could tell he loved the idea.

Traffic hummed in the background, and the line of cars to the drive-up coffee shop dwindled. As the clock crept up on six, fewer people wanted another shot of espresso, regardless of how bad traffic was.

She surrendered to the desire to constantly know what time it was and pulled up her email. The feedback, rejections, and requests were trickling in from the queries she'd sent out. The rejections still stung, but none had brought her to tears yet like the first one, and the encouragement was enough to fuel her. Nothing had gone further than initial interest yet, but she was hopeful.

A familiar pickup pulled into the parking lot, and she kept her attention on her phone, pretending not to notice but unable to hide her relieved smile. Zero of her focus was on the message in front of her. Instead, she was on full alert, listening to the approaching footsteps.

"I think your coffee got cold." She tried to sound irritated when she knew Zane was within earshot.

He crouched in front of her, placed one hand on either side of her face, and pressed his lips to hers. She closed her eyes and sank into the kiss with a tiny sigh, flushed when he pulled away.

"I'm more worried that I kept you waiting than about the temperature of my coffee." He dropped onto the bench next to her, arm pressed against hers. "I'm so sorry I'm late. The one day rush-hour traffic is a bitch in this valley has to be one that matters."

"I guess I'll forgive you today." She leaned her head against his shoulder.

He brushed his lips over her forehead. "You're generous like that. I'll make sure to let the other commuters know you'll be irritated if they hold me up in the future."

She laughed and shifted in her seat so she could see him, but not enough to break the contact. "How was your first day of work?"

He tried to give her a casual shrug, but the smile that threatened to break out told her he thought he was about to be funny. "My boss is an asshole slave driver."

She sighed and rolled her eyes. She had heard

Scott use that line more times than she cared to count.

"What?" He looked miffed. "I thought it was funny."

"Yeah, so does he." She tried to sound irritated at having someone new repeat the line, but she couldn't keep her smile off her face.

"I get paid to laugh at it, so I'll think it's funny for longer."

She shook her head. "That's not what you get paid for, but I'm glad you have a new boyfriend."

He stuck out his tongue at her. She poked the tip with her finger, and he sucked it back in. She kissed him deeply, loving the tingle it sent through her and the pressure of his hand against the small of her back.

"How did it really go?" she asked when they broke apart.

"It's too early to tell, but so far so good." He paused for a moment, as if considering his next words. "I got to have lunch with the boss's wife. Didn't know that was a perk. I think you'd like her. She's almost as sexy as you, but kind of uptight. She reminded me a lot of you."

She nudged his shoulder with hers, not able to stop laughing. "You're being a dork. Why did you have lunch with Kenzie, and why didn't you invite me?"

"It was a private meeting. I needed her opinion on something."

A sliver of doubt wormed through her. Why was he keeping secrets? It had to be nothing; she trusted him. Besides, if it involved Kenzie, it had to be okay. She pushed the uncertainty away. Only way to find out was to ask. They were done not speaking up. "Do I get to know what about?"

He drummed his fingers on the table. "What do you think she'd say if she knew how many ways we'd abused her Ethan Allen dining set?"

"She'd be horrified, especially if we scratched the finish."

He shrugged. "I was hoping she'd give it to us as a wedding gift. We get more use out of it than she does."

The sentiment warmed her, but she didn't dwell. Part of her assumed marriage was an eventuality, but there was no reason to push it. "She's rich now, so she'd better buy us a not-used gift when that day comes." *If.* She'd meant to say if. Not *when.* Oops. Too late to take it back now.

He drummed his fingers faster. "I'm sorry I don't have any candles. Or champagne. Or violin music."

She looked at him, not hiding her confusion. "Um… I'm not worried about it?"

"I really hope Kenzie was right. And the same size."

She shook her head and blinked, trying to make sense of his half-sentences. "Is it just me, or are you babbling?"

He slid from the bench and dropped to one knee, and her heart leaped into her throat. The fake proposal from a few weeks earlier came rushing back, taunting her. This was going to get old fast if he kept doing it. She clenched her jaw, not wanting to hope, but unable to help herself.

He grasped her fingers in his. "Riley Ann

Carter"—a nervous tremor ran through his voice—"you are the most beautiful, brilliant, and incredible person I've ever met." He pulled a small box from his pocket, and her heart flipped in on itself. "I don't know what I would do without you in my life." He locked his gaze on hers, his sincerity distinct in his eyes. "So I'm hoping—" He swallowed and opened the box. A simple band with a stunning diamond setting winked back at her. "I'm hoping you'll do me the honor of becoming my wife."

"Yes." The answer was out before she could think about it. She didn't *need* to think about it; she already knew. She bent over and kissed him hard, memorizing the moment, burning every single detail into her memory. "Yes, and a million times *yes* again."

He slid the ring on her finger, and it nestled perfectly into place. Having a twin had advantages she'd never realized. "Kenzie really helped you pick this out?"

He shook his head. "She let me borrow her finger for sizing. I already knew which one you wanted."

Of course he did. She never should have doubted it. She pulled him to his feet. "I didn't think they still made this design."

He tugged her up. "It was in the retro settings. Apparently, we're retro now."

"I don't care what they call it." She draped her arms around his neck, snuggling close, focusing on every inch of him and the way they molded together. "I love it. I love you."

He nipped her earlobe and hooked his thumbs

in her back pockets. "So, in case your sister doesn't let us keep the table, want to give it one more spin?"

She laughed and tilted her head back, loving it when his soft lips found the hollow at the base of her throat.

His words vibrated against her skin. "I'm going to assume that means *yes*."

The End

If you'd like to see what happens when hacker meets hacker idol, check out Jared and Mikki's book, *His Hacker*. Keep reading for a free sneak peek of chapter one

his hacker

chapter one

Jared's fingers twitched toward the slew of jumbled shot glasses on the shelf in front of him. He shouldn't be browsing the gift shop of the hotel he was staying in; he should be on the same conference call as his best friend and business associate, helping to wrap up the biggest sale they'd had in their sights in months. He could have listened in. Just this once. Kept himself on mute and not said anything.

Compulsion won out, and he turned back to the shelf of shot glasses. His fingers flew across the rims and, within seconds, the entire section was a series of straight, neat lines.

He exhaled loudly. Okay, so maybe he couldn't have listened quietly on the phone and kept his mouth shut.

And none of this junk would make a good souvenir for his sister. She'd asked for something simple, but everyone brought back tiny trinkets from Las Vegas. He was halfway to the gift shop exit when a tucked-away display caught his attention. The digital photo frames were tacky as hell, trimmed with gaudy, gold Greek temples, and was that supposed to be a crown of leaves? Alyssia's entire desk was lined with photos. It was perfect.

Great. A line at the checkout. His toes tapped a tuneless beat inside his shoes as he waited for his turn to pay. At least waiting would give him something else to think about for a couple of seconds longer.

He couldn't help checking his watch as he stepped from the store. He'd killed six minutes and fifty-four seconds.

Tate, Vivian, and he would be heading to dinner as soon as the call was done. His associates were staying in the same hotel. But until then, Jared's schedule was open. *Time to sequester myself in my room and get some work done.* He'd get back to the proposal sitting in his briefcase for new call center hardware. Answer the emails with red exclamation points on them that had come in during his flight.

His gaze tripped around the lobby as he pulled out his phone and unlocked it. People came and went. The couple checking in, she with silver hair cropped short, he in jeans and a T-shirt and probably thirty years younger, spent more time gazing at each other than looking at anyone else. Even across the room their adoration was almost tangible.

Too bad it won't last. People never took the time to figure out their own oddities before they hooked up with another person, but over the years, he'd managed to assemble a solid algorithm of what did and didn't work for him when considering a personal relationship.

He didn't expect perfection from a significant other, but there was no reason the relationship couldn't be flawless. The math was there to support it, as long as the variables were right. In a way it was harsh, but it hadn't let him down yet.

A twinge of envy echoed in his chest as he pulled his attention away from the loving couple, aka pending heartbreak. His eyes grew wide when his gaze landed on the woman whose black hair—complete with a Kool-Aid red streak down one side—just brushed her jaw.

Back to your hotel room. Work awaits. But the woman had his attention, and his feet refused to move. Even from this distance, she screamed *chaos* in a way that made his fingers twitch with the need to bring order. And at the same time, he couldn't stop staring.

Her hot pink T-shirt draped off one shoulder, exposing a strap of the black tank top underneath, and her messenger bag hugged her body enough to highlight perky breasts and round hips. Her lips moved as her gaze traveled the tablet in her hands. She glanced up occasionally when she swiped the screen, and then went back to whatever had her so engrossed.

Beautiful. The thought caught him off guard. It was true, her face was attractive and her bag enhanced every seductive curve, but something else had captivated him. He studied her a little longer as she shuffled at half-speed toward an unknown destination. It was the intensity she read her tablet with. Her gaze and focus were enthralling.

Being able to pay attention was an important quality in any individual. Not that he was keeping track. Even if his thoughts were taunting him with images of stripping her shirt off and exploring her bare skin. He had way too much work to do this trip to deal with something like base lust.

He turned toward the elevator.

He exhaled as he stepped into a waiting car. *Don't think about the call. You've got other work to do. Like making sure this sale and the next aren't repeats of those in the past.*

His eyes grew wide when the woman with the tablet stepped through the closing doors, only looking up long enough to push a number on the control panel. The elevator sealed them off from the rest of the world, and she continued to stare at the device in her hands.

What's she reading that's so fascinating? He inched a step closer and peered over her shoulder. The faint scent of citrus teased him and kicked his pulse up a notch. His mouth twisted in ambivalence when he saw what had her attention. "You know none of that's accurate, right?"

He hid his wince. This was why he didn't talk to anyone on sales calls except the technical people.

She spun, eyes almost as dark as the eyeliner rimming them taking a moment to focus on his face. Her confusion vanished in a smirk.

"Which bit of it?" Between words, she clacked something against her teeth. A barbell—she had her tongue pierced. There was absolutely nothing logical about the accessory. But knowing as much didn't stop the blood from draining from his head and racing toward his lower extremities. She traced the metal ball along the back of her teeth, gaze never leaving his face.

His thoughts teased him with images of what it would be like to feel the piercing in other places, and his cock twitched in response. *Down, boy. Don't go there.* "The entire article." She hadn't balked at his comment. Might as well push the subject.

She glanced at the device in her hands, as if she'd forgotten it was there, and then back at him.

Completely captivating gaze.

"I think you're being a bit extreme." She tapped her nails on the edge of the frame, attention locked on him. "You can't tell me things like gateways, the NSA, and the deep web don't exist."

A shimmer of appreciation pinged inside him. She was reading tech and had been absorbed by it. *Sexy.* He couldn't think of a better word for it. Except it didn't make the information any more correct.

"I'm not saying they don't exist. Just not in that capacity. It's a sensationalist article meant to strike an irrational fear into people." He knew better than to unleash his unfiltered thoughts on the general public, but something about the challenge in her expression told him she didn't mind. It wasn't as though he was trying to extend the conversation. Or maybe he was just a little.

The car came to a stop, and the door slid open on what he assumed was her floor. Attention never leaving his face, she reached behind her and pressed the *Door Open* button. "That's the point."

He needed to cut this conversation short. Too

bad his mouth didn't agree. "To read something that's wrong?"

She dropped her tablet into her messenger bag, eyes never leaving his for more than a few seconds. "Someone obviously thinks it's true. Which means there's value in being able to plainly state why it's not possible, and knowing if it actually is."

"But that's why computers are fantastic. Only so many possibilities exist, and the things they mention in the article—" he nodded at her tablet, "—aren't on the list."

"Not yet, anyway. I love this place, you know?"

The circuits in his head tripped and stumbled, trying to keep up with the conversation. Time to regain control. "I'm not seeing the connection to the *Wired* article."

"No connection. It's my first time here, so I'm still awestruck. It's amazing, right? All the lights, the people, the energy."

Now he had enough information to switch tracks and fall back into the discussion. "It's fixed odds, careless dreams, and when it's light outside, really dirty."

What was wrong with him? Besides the fact he couldn't get a handle on this woman and his fantasy was still running rampant, having now stripped her down to her panties. Did she taste like the faint lemon and plum drifting off her? *None of those thoughts are logical. Get a grip.*

"Once again, that's the point." Enthusiasm shone in her eyes as she talked. "It's a chance to experience things that aren't a part of everyday life. For instance, how many of those couples downstairs will only spend the one night together and then never see each other again?" She ducked her head as the question trailed off, but not before he saw the red flush her cheeks. "Sorry. I get carried away. Guys like you probably have more important things on their minds."

The alarm on the door protested at being held open so long. A part of his brain said the sound was another hint it was time to cut things short. *Soon.*

"Guys like me?" One thing he never did was one-night stands. But just then, studying each move and gesture and fighting a raging hard-on at the thought of trailing his fingers over her bare skin, he wondered if she was on to something.

She met his gaze again. "Jared Tippins, Director of Information Technology for Skriddie Bust Media, and world-renowned network security genius."

An uncomfortable chill crept through him, and he shook it off. She could have recited that off his business card, it was so eerily succinct and accurate. Except the bit about being a security genius. That was implied. Was he supposed to know her? Great, he was fantasizing about screwing a prospective client or something. But he would have remembered her. "We haven't met."

"Not really." She extended the hand not holding the elevator open. "I'm Mikki."

Which didn't clear anything up, but did give a name to his out-of-control thoughts. The strain against his jeans had already passed uncomfortable. When her warm, smooth palm nestled in his, it only got worse.

Something hummed in his jeans' pocket. He dragged himself out of his own head, forcing away the arousal and trying to shake off the disorienting cobwebs left by the fantasy.

She nodded at his waist, playful smirk dancing on her lips, and leaned in close enough to whisper, "You're vibrating."

The heat brushing his skin, her teasing voice, and those full lips… He was seconds from suggesting they take this back to her room so he could add some reality to the fantasy. Except, even if she wasn't everything chaotic and unpredictable, that was his work phone, and no one was buzzing him this late unless it was critical.

"Duty calls." He gave her an apologetic smile.

"Enjoy work." She laughed lightly and spun on her toe. "See you around," she called over her shoulder.

It took the last of his willpower to drag his gaze from her ass before the elevator doors cut off his view. It wasn't the round shape, or the hint of wiggle—though both were incredible. It was the bounce in her step. *Right. Work. Back to it.*

His creeping good mood sank with the extra gravity of the rising elevator when he saw the text from Tate. He rubbed his forehead to chase away the tension, but a headache still threatened at the simple note. *Dial in. Now.*

That was a bad sign. Jared reached his floor, headed toward his room, and pulled up the info in his calendar. He was already calling before he slid the keycard in the lock. Tate wanted him there to finalize details; that was all. *If only I believed it.*

Jared swiped in the call pin and dropped into the chair in front of the desk in his room—alone. Regret murmured in his thoughts. *How can I be so disappointed about letting someone I just met run off?*

The line clicked into a conversation already in progress, and it took a few seconds for his ears to adjust to the speaker's heavy accent. It was why the call was happening after business hours. Skriddie specialized in electronic security for retail stores, and this potential client was overseas, building sites for a wide variety of companies. That was what made the sale so big—they had dozens of customer sites that would need to be verified, tested, and put through the wringer. All of them worth millions, and most of them high-profile.

As an independent third party, Skriddie would be responsible for certifying that each site, and all the customer information contained there, was safe from hackers.

Tate cut through a pause in the dialogue. "I think someone just joined the call."

"Good evening, or morning, everyone. This is Jared Tippins, director of technology for Skriddie Bust Media." He kept his tone light and friendly, despite the anxious march dancing through every limb. "I'm sorry I'm late." Which was ridiculous, since he wasn't originally invited, but professionalism was what it was. Easy enough to remember, now that the blood wasn't rushing away from his brain.

"Glad you could join us." It was unlikely anyone on the call had heard the tension in Tate's greeting, but after almost three decades of friendship, Jared knew how bad a sign it was. "We just have some questions for you before we finalize everything—"

"*If* we finalize anything," someone corrected him.

Jared snarled silently at the receiver, glad no one on the phone could see him. He swallowed his retort and kept his mouth shut, waiting for more details.

"Right, of course." Tate's chuckle sounded like it had been strained through a cheese grater. "Jared, we have their head developer with us, so feel free to get as technical as you need to address their concerns."

Which, Jared knew from experience, didn't mean he could get technical at all. He'd have to walk a fine line between letting the developers know he was knowledgeable, and not boring anyone else listening in.

And then the questions began. Five minutes in, Jared's grasp on not getting too in depth slipped. After ten minutes, he tossed all filters by the roadside as he was assaulted with some of the most obscure, low-level questions he'd ever encountered. Ranging from things that hadn't been an issue since the internet was born, to little-known, cutting-edge techniques he knew almost no one had dared implement yet.

He handled it all, the entire time curious about where the third degree had come from and confident he answered every concern with zero error margin.

"Jared." He recognized the voice at this point as

their developer. "Do you test for all these possible holes in your own network?"

Jared choked down a sarcastic laugh. Did he monitor his own systems for weaknesses no one had heard of in a decade, or wouldn't be familiar with for at least six more months? "Of course we do. We conduct internal audits on a regular basis, and my staff is encouraged to keep current on any and all new developments in the technology industry."

The muscles in his neck tightened, and the beginning of an ache throbbed behind his temples. This was too much like the other two lost sales they'd been sure they'd had in the bag. Both contracts lost to NetSafe Systems. He clenched and unclenched his free hand. And Jared was almost convinced NSS was behind whatever was leading to these lines of questions.

At first he and his colleagues at Skriddie tried to convince themselves it was just sour grapes, that they were pissed off NSS was owning their pitches so much better. But the pattern was too familiar. Every time Skriddie competed with the other company for a client, the question of internal network security came up.

But at least that meant Jared could anticipate the next question and could head off the concern before anyone asked. His network was perfect, and he was certain of that. Time to restore some confidence. "We have copies of those internal and independent system audits. We, of course, would never expect you to put your faith in someone who doesn't hold themselves to the same security standards as their clients. I'll send them to the group as soon as this call is finished."

"We'd appreciate that, thank you." That would be one of their executives.

"Fantastic." The dash of stress still flavored Tate's reply. "So if no one has further questions, we can have the contract ready for you tonight and schedule a kickoff meeting for early next week."

"I think we'd like to hold off on that," another of their managers said. "We still have significant concerns and need time to discuss our options internally while we conduct due diligence."

"Of course." Tate's tone was too cheerful. "Let us know if we can answer any more questions at all. We're here for you."

Jared muted his phone and kept silent as they exchanged pleasantries and wrapped up. *Due diligence my ass. There's nothing to see.* The moment he disconnected, he let out the roar of frustration that had been building in his chest for several minutes. It echoed harmlessly off the surrounding walls.

The pattern was exactly the same as the last two times. That wouldn't stop him from sending off the information he'd promised. But experience told him it wasn't going to matter.

Email sent, he dialed Tate and started talking as soon as the line clicked on. "We're fucked. You know that, right?"

"Intimately." The phony professionalism had vanished from Tate's voice. "You with V?"

Vivian, their counterpart from operations, was still in her room working. "No."

"So she doesn't know yet. Lucky her." Tate's

sigh clattered over the receiver. "I say we grab a taxi and find a local place where we can get so drunk we forget this happened until tomorrow morning when NSS rubs our noses in it."

"We can't." Jared didn't know where Tate had gotten the notion taking the night off was a good idea. "We have to track this down."

"You've vetted this rumor five billion times already." Tate sounded exhausted. "Staying up all night for the five billion and first time looking for something that doesn't exist won't do you any good."

"You want answers as much as I do." Jared let the irritation leak into his retort. "If the rumors are still out there, we've missed something."

"What are you going to check that you haven't yet?"

"I'll figure that out when I get there." Finding answers was just as important to his friend. Then again, Tate had a point. They didn't know where to look next. He could drag this conversation out for the next half hour, or concede, and search for solutions while he tried to unwind. If he was going to yield, he was doing it on his terms.

"All right." Jared relented. "I'll ping Viv and then get a recommendation from the concierge."

"That was too easy. We're *not* doing karaoke."

Jared smiled at the phone. Music was his one outlet. People said it was an artistic medium, but he knew better. A good, solid song followed the same methodology as a well-written software program. There was a math to it. Only so many right answers and a series of patterns that made it pleasant and functional.

Tate was welcome to get wasted. But Jared needed a new angle to approach this problem from, and this was how he wanted to let his mind wander. "Yeah, we are."

"Pfft. Then V and I are picking your songs."

"Fine with me. Meet us in the lobby in five." Jared dialed Vivian the moment the call disconnected.

Maybe he should have chased down miss hot-pink T-shirt Mikki, who had the gorgeous eyes. At least then he'd have some satisfaction to go along with the feeling he'd just been fucked.

The story continues in chapter two…